走近动物系列（中英文版）

ANIMAL LEGENDS—CIVILIZATION

韦　诚　李益芳◎编著
李　雪◎译

动物的文明传奇

北京师范大学出版集团
BEIJING NORMAL UNIVERSITY PUBLISHING GROUP
安徽大学出版社

图书在版编目(CIP)数据

动物的文明传奇:汉英对照/韦诚,李益芳编著. —合肥:安徽大学出版社,2017.3
(走近动物系列)
ISBN 978-7-5664-1387-1

Ⅰ. ①动… Ⅱ. ①韦… ②李… Ⅲ. ①英语—汉语—对照读物②故事—作品集—中国—当代 Ⅳ. ①H319.4:I

中国版本图书馆 CIP 数据核字(2017)第 060184 号

动物的文明传奇　　韦　诚　李益芳　编著

出版发行: 北京师范大学出版集团
安 徽 大 学 出 版 社
(安徽省合肥市肥西路 3 号 邮编 230039)
www.bnupg.com.cn
www.ahupress.com.cn

印　　刷: 安徽昶颉包装印务有限责任公司
经　　销: 全国新华书店
开　　本: 130mm×184mm
印　　张: 6.75
字　　数: 152 千字
版　　次: 2017 年 3 月第 1 版
印　　次: 2017 年 3 月第 1 次印刷
定　　价: 27.00 元
ISBN 978-7-5664-1387-1

策划编辑: 李　梅　唐洪全　　**装帧设计:** 丁　健
责任编辑: 李　雪　姚树君　　**美术编辑:** 李　军
责任印制: 赵明炎

动物：人类的镜子

——走近动物系列（中英文版）序

对其他生命的尊重正是对人类生命的关注；解放动物，就是解放人类自己。

——彼得·辛格（英国）

Respect for other kinds of lives is attention to human lives; the liberation of animals means liberation of mankind itself.

—Peter Singer (Britain)

走近动物系列（中英文版）由《动物的爱情传奇》《动物的文明传奇》《动物的战争传奇》和《动物的义举传奇》四个分册组成。翻开扉页，书中妙趣横生的传奇，生动鲜活的图片，富有哲理的点评，将带您进入神奇的动物王国。

当我们为人类五千年的文明感到自豪和骄傲的时候，您是否意识到，在生命的进化过程中，尽管有优与劣、高与低的区分，但永远难以否认这样一个事实：地球上的每一种生命体，都会自觉或不自觉地，这样或那样地去营

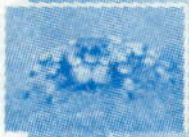

建某种属于自己的物质世界和精神家园。恩格斯在《反杜林论》中指出："人类来源于动物界这一事实已经决定人类永远不能摆脱兽性。所以，问题永远只能在于摆脱得多些或少些，在于兽性和人性程度上的差异。"从这一认识出发，人们要实现对自身最本源、最本质的认识，解开动物世界的谜团，走近动物世界，是一个绝好的选择。

随着人们对环境和生态平衡认识的深入，人与动物的平等和谐相处也日益得到认同。很多过去在我们看来只有人才有的行为，在动物世界也是屡见不鲜。德国慕尼黑动物园内有一条九个月大的雌性章鱼居然会用"手"打开玻璃瓶盖，吃掉瓶内的虾蟹。北京西直门桥有只喜鹊经常和人逗乐。人们怎么逗它玩都可以，只要你伸手去捉，它一下就飞走了。多么富有人情味的动物啊！保护动物权益运动的倡导者美国普林斯顿大学哲学教授彼得·辛格认为，动物应该享受同人类一样的权益，因为它们同样具有生理和心理感受。但是，人与动物到底如何平等，是一个永恒的哲学课题。我们不应该完全按照人的标准去给动物划分善恶标准，更不能随便处置，甚至消灭某种动物，人为砍断生物链。

人和动物也有很多和谐相处的佳话。生活在南极洲的企鹅，同人类就非常友好，当它们看到船只靠岸时，就一个个迅速从水中出来，集拢在一起，排成整齐的队伍，昂首企望，高高兴兴地迎接客人。它们身披黑色"斗篷"，

内穿白色“衣裤”，形态活泼，情景动人。要是你坐在岩石和冰块上休息，它有时还会悄悄走过来，用嘴亲吻你的衣角，甚至还可能衔一块五颜六色的光滑美丽的石子送给你。顾兵是昆明世博园的一位管理人员，因能零距离亲近红嘴鸥而被誉为“鸥王”。人们常常可以看到红嘴鸥在顾兵的头上“漫步”、从嘴中“夺食”和手中啄食，尽享与红嘴鸥和谐共处的欢乐。

在一些文学作品中，也有关于人和动物之间美好而真挚的友情描述。如《失落的童心》一文，作者一直都很难忘怀童年时爷爷家里养过的那几只羊：“每次到爷爷家中，总有两只活泼可爱的小羔羊如雪团般，迎我而来，见到我总是围着我蹦蹦跳跳团团转，又是扯我的衣襟，又是舔我的小手，哪怕是一日之隔，它们也会用同样的方式来欢迎我。它们乖巧俏皮的模样自然也赢来了同龄小伙伴们的喜爱。两只小羊似乎已是我们当中的成员。”在很多场合，人和动物都是可以和谐相处的。2004 年 9 月 13 日上午，在河南平顶山市东安路北段一蜂产品专卖店前，全身爬满 5 万余只蜜蜂的王俊，同蜜蜂可谓是亲密无间。他从 1975 年起开始帮助姐夫养蜂，一次他从蜂巢中掏出老蜂王放入小笼子挂在树下，几个小时后，发现几万只蜜蜂扑在笼子外不走。后来，他知道蜂王身上能够分泌出一种特殊的气体，与其相处长久的蜜蜂就会跟着它身上的气体走。于是他开始训练蜜蜂，所以他走到哪里蜜蜂

就能跟到哪里。

人类为了保护动物做了大量的工作。为挽救濒临灭绝的生物物种，日本制造了一个专门冷冻保存生物细胞和基因的设施——“时间密封舱”。在这个“时间密封舱”里建有14个冷冻箱，可以在液态氮中把样本冷冻到零下150摄氏度，保存50年以上。密封舱主要保存从濒危生物活体中采集的皮肤组织和从尸体中采取的脏器和生殖细胞等。目前，在日本，200种以上有灭绝危险的鸟类、哺乳类、鱼类等生物都将成为密封舱的保存对象。在未来，日本科研人员可以利用冷冻保存的资源进行物种生命还原计划，比如，哺乳类动物利用克隆技术还原。鸟类可以采取在近亲种类的蛋里注入灭绝鸟类的生殖细胞来还原，鱼类也可采取与之相似的方法还原。

亲近自然和动物是人与生俱来的本性。在现实生活中，许多人亲近动物，甚至将它们视为自己的家庭成员，而宠物反过来也能满足人心理和生理上的各种需求。生理学和心理学研究显示，有宠物陪伴的儿童，认知能力和社交能力比普通孩子更容易培养。在同宠物相处的过程中，孩子的表达能力和责任感逐步会得到提高，更容易同小环境中的其他成员和谐相处。有宠物的老人，往往能更加乐观地对待生活，珍惜现在和将来。

动物给人类带来快乐和祥和的同时，也给人类带来了战争和毁灭。《汉书》记载了许多由蝗灾引发的战争。

例如，公元前130年秋天，蝗虫遮天蔽日之后，禾苗已空；民不聊生，饥荒四起，瘟疫流行，饥民四处逃难；皇帝便派四名大将掠夺南越。类似记载，在中国的历史典籍中可谓“史不绝书”。人们都知道第一次世界大战爆发的原因是帝国主义列强之间矛盾的激化，并以1914年6月28日奥匈帝国皇储Franz Ferdinand在塞尔维亚被暗杀为导火索。但人们也许不知道这一行刺活动却与一种昆虫有关。美国昆虫学家M. T. Smulyan(1920年)在昆虫杂志*Psych*里用文学家的语言以“一种昆虫和缺乏昆虫知识——一个世界大战的直接原因”为题向我们展示了大致的轮廓。他写道：在塞尔维亚内地的一个村庄里有个小伙子发疯般地爱上了同村的一位姑娘。姑娘养了一只漂亮的小鸟，她把这只鸟看得比生命都珍贵。正当她准备接受小伙子的爱的时候，一种寄生性昆虫夺走了小鸟的生命。脆弱的姑娘深深为之悲伤，不久便也染病死去。此事使小伙子精神上受到很大挫折，他几近疯狂，离开了村庄，不久便在塞尔维亚的另一个地方加入了一个极为爱国的革命组织。紧接着，他在萨拉热窝暗杀了奥地利的皇储，从而导致了1914年7月28日奥匈帝国向塞尔维亚宣战。一周之内德、俄、法、英等相继投入战争，第一次世界大战就这样拉开了序幕。

走近动物系列(中英文版)里所描述的每一个故事虽然都是孤立的，但当我们将这些故事进行科学归纳和分类后却发现，每一个故事所表达的爱恨情仇同人类社会是那样的异曲同工。动物世界的自然法则和生存法则对于人类社会来说，是一部简洁易懂的生命哲学教科书。

亲爱的朋友！翻开图文并茂、装帧精美、视觉独特的走近动物系列（中英文版），通过一个又一个生动鲜活的动物故事，你一定会对自然、社会和人类的和谐发展有更多的领悟。你也一定能在奇趣盎然的动物王国旅行中，发现真理，感悟人生。同时，书中翔实生动地记载和独特科学的分类也为动物学、心理学、生物学、人类学、管理学、法学和哲学等的研究提供了可资借鉴的素材。

The collection of *Approaching Animals* constitutes 4 volumes, namely, *Animal Legends—Romances*, *Animal legends—Civilization*, *Animal Legends—Wars*, *Animal Legends—Heroes*. Open the books and you will be ushered in to the amazing kingdom of animals by the legends full of wit and humor, the pictures full of freshness and aliveness, and the comments full of philosophic insights in the book.

When we are proud of the thousands of years of the history of mankind, do we for a moment realize that: although there is difference between the strong and the weak, the high and the low in the evolution of lives, but a fact can never be neglected—every living thing on the planet will consciously or subconsciously build a material world and spiritual home belonging to itself in one way or another. In *Anti-Dühring*, Engels pointed out: "The fact that mankind originates from the animal world determines that mankind can never get rid of their animal nature. Therefore, the question only lies in the extent to which mankind get rid of it, and in the difference between animal nature and human nature in their degrees." From this statement, we can judge that to approach the animal world and solve its mysteries is a best way to acquire the most ultimate and most fundamental understanding of mankind.

As our knowledge of the environment and ecological equilibrium deepens, the equal and harmonious co-existence of human beings with animals gets more approval. Many acts which we have regarded as human-specific turn out to be common occurrences in the animal world. There was a nine-month-old female octopus in a zoo in German which knew to open the lid of a glass bottle with its "hands" and then eat the shrimps and crabs inside. There was a cuckoo bird in Beijing which liked teasing people and would fly away the moment there was someone who attempted to catch it. How

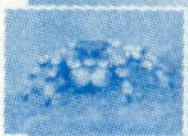

human-like these animals are! Peter Singer, Professor of Philosophy of Princeton University in the US, who is a pioneer in the movement of protecting animal rights, holds that animals should enjoy the same rights as human beings because they possess the same mental and physical feeling as humans do. However, it remains an everlasting philosophical question of how equality could be realized between human beings and animals. We should not judge animals good or bad completely according to our own standards. We should not dispose of, or even eradicate some animal kinds and break apart the biologic chain.

There are also many much-praised stories of harmonious co-existence between humans and animals. Penguins living in the Antarctica are very friendly towards humans. When they see an approaching boat, they will quickly come out of the water one by one, gather together and form an orderly formation, look up in expectation and welcome the guests in happiness. They are dressed in black "cloaks" and white "clothes", making a much lively and interesting scene. If you are resting on a rock or an ice block, sometimes they will come over quietly and kiss the corners of your clothes

with their beaks, or even bring you a colorful, smooth and beautiful pebble as a present. There is a staff in Kunming Expo Park named Gu who is also named "king of black-headed gulls" because he can get close contacts with them. Gu is often observed to be harmoniously playing with the black-headed gulls. Sometimes they are walking on his head, other times they will snatch food from his hands or even his mouth.

There are also descriptions of beautiful and sincere friendships between humans and animals in some literature works. In the Lost Childlike Innocence, the author often recalls the several sheep raised by his grandpa in his childhood. "every time I came to grandpa, there were also two lovely and lively little lambs coming to welcome me, jumping about to welcome my presence. They would pull my clothes or lick my little hands. Even I have been absent for just one day, they would nonetheless welcome me in the same style. Their cute and smart looks naturally won the love of my peers and they seem to be a group member among us."

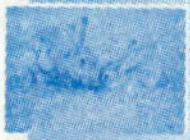

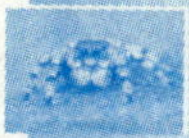

On many occasions, harmonious relationship can be realized between humans and animals. On the morning of September 13, 2004, Wang was working in front of a shop for honey product with more than 50,000 bees on him. It seemed that the bees and he were as thick as thieves. He started to help his brother-in-law in raising bees since 1975. One day, he took the queen bee and hung it in a little cage under a tree. Several hours later he found thousands of bees flying around the cage and would not go away. Later he learned that the queen bee can produce a particular scent which would draw the bees living for a long time with it. From then on he started to train bees to the extent that they would follow him anywhere he goes.

In order to protect animals, mankind have done a considerable amount of works. The Japanese made a facility specially—" the time-sealing capsule "—for freezing-preservation of biological cells and genes in order to save endangered species. There were 14 cooling chambers in the "time-sealing" capsule which could freeze samples to −150 ℃ in liquid nitrogen and preserve them to up to 50 years. The capsule mainly preserved skin tissues collected from the living bodies of endangered species, as well as organs and germ cells from corpses. Currently in Japan, more than 200

endangered birds, mammals and fishes will be listed as protected objects of the capsule. In the future, Japanese researchers can use the freezing-preserved resources for carrying out the plan for restoration of species' lives. For example, mammals can be restored in cloning, birds could be restored by injection of the germ cells of endangered birds into the eggs of a close relative, and fishes can also be restored following similar methods.

Love for nature and animals is an intrinsic human nature. In real life, many people are close to animals and even regard them as their own family members. In return, pets can also satisfy various mental and physical needs of mankind. As shown in studies of physiology and psychology, children accompanied by pets are easier in their cultivation of cognitive and social abilities than normal children. In the process of getting along with pets, the ability of expression and sense of responsibility would be enhanced in children. They would find it easier to get along with other members in a small environment. An old person accompanied by pets tends to treat life with more optimism and he or she may cherish the present and the future more.

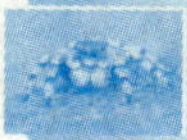

Just as animals can bring happiness and harmony to

mankind, they also bring warfare and destruction. *The History of the Han Dynasty* records many wars triggered by locust plagues. For example, in the autumn of 130 BC, after a severe locust plague, there was no crop in the fields. The masses had no means to leave. Famine and plague spread along with their victims everywhere. The emperor they dispatched 4 generals to loot the areas. Similar records are too numerous to be listed in the books of history of China.

We all know that the reason for the breaking out of World War I is the intensification of conflicts among imperialist powers and that it was triggered by the assassination of the heir apparent of Austro Hungary—Franz Ferdinand—in Serbia. But we do not know that the assassination had to do with a kind of insect. American entomologist M. T. Smulyan wrote in a magazine of insects using a much literary title "a kind of insect and lack of knowledge about the insect—the direct reason for World War I": In a village in Serbia, a lad fell in love with a lass like crazy. The lass kept a beautiful little bird as pet and valued it more than her life. Just as the lass was about to accept the love of the lad, a parasite insect took the life of the little bird and

the weak lass was deeply stricken. She took to her bed and died not long after. The lad undergone therefore undergone a severe mental shock and left the village in half insanity. He later joined an extra-patriotic revolutionary organization in another place in Serbia and joined the heir apparent of Austro Hungary in Sarajevo, which assassination led to the declaration of war of Austro Hungary against Serbia. Within a week, German, Russia, France and Britain attended the war and World War I thus began.

Although each story in the series of *Approaching Animals* (Chinese and English editions) is independent, as we generalize and classify these stories we will find that the needs of instinct and all kinds of feelings expressed in each story are much similar to those in human society. The law of nature and rules of living presented in the animal world are really a textbook of the philosophy of life concise and simple to understand for human society.

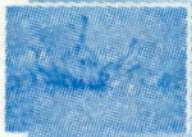

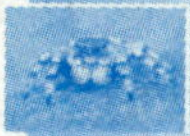

Dear readers! When you open the richly-illustrated, beautifully-bound series of *Approaching Animals* (Chinese and English editions) with their unique visual effects, when you read these live and fresh animal stories one after another, you will surly acquire more insights into the harmonious development between nature, society and mankind! Also, one can definitely discover the truth and understand life in the tour into the animal kingdom abundant in interest. In the meantime, the detailed and accurate recording as well as the unique and scientific classification also provides materials for reference for studies of zoology, psychology, biology, anthropology, management science, law and philosophy.

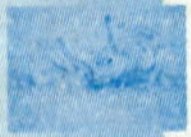

前　言

文明，生命智慧的结晶。它往往被理解为人类社会的进步状态，是人类特有的精神现象。然而，据生物学家的长期考察和研究，发现世界上有不少动物和人类一样，作为一种生命的存在形式，同样会用自己特有的方式创造一种只属于自己的文明。法国小说家普鲁斯特在《走进非洲》一书中说过："最特别的旅行，便是透过别人的眼睛，观看同一熟悉的地方。但也许透过其他物种的眼睛来反观人类，我们才能在滚滚堕落洪流中，偶尔瞥见一丝一毫的良善。"

动物世界的文明相对人类的文明虽然是低级的，但是，毕竟有不少动物能够制造工具和进行语言交流，甚至它们还有自己的语言大师和音乐家。同时，在它们的群体生活中，也有许多"文明"现象同人类的"精神文明建设"有异曲同工之妙。"团结互助"的螃蟹在蜕壳时，常常成群结队地趴在一起。那些已长好硬壳的螃蟹自动担负起哨兵的职责，在洞外放哨，保护正在蜕壳的同伴免受侵害。在美洲沙漠地带有一种"有福同享"的蜜蚁，当它遇到含有蜜汁的食物时就美美地饱餐一顿，然后"满载而归"。当遇见没吃到此类食物的同伴时，它就会主动从口里吐出蜜汁让其分享，有时甚至自己变得腹中空空也"毫

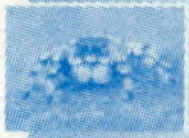

无怨言”。在非洲多哥的拉拉斯山上，生活着一种“善解人意”的“礼貌鸟”。这种鸟头尖、身圆、尾长，全身长着绿色羽毛。它们常常飞进村子，将嘴里衔着的东西投向村民或投进住宅窗口。这些东西不是香气扑鼻的野花，就是鲜美可口的果子，人们在接受这些“礼物”后，就用谷粒或豆子款待它们。礼貌鸟的记忆力很强，所到之处，谁对它友好，它就经常“光临”，反之，它就不再上门了。无独有偶，在热带森林中有一种“热情好客”的鹦鹉，不仅同族间互相友爱，而且对其他鸟类也十分好客。如果它们在林中聚餐时，看见有其他鸟类飞来，就会热情高唱“迎宾曲”，邀请“客人”光临，共进美餐。在浩渺的海洋中，沙丁鱼也懂得“敬老爱幼”。沙丁鱼群在海中遨游时，从不争先恐后挤成一团，若游到特别狭窄的地方，总是让年幼者在上层，年长者在下层，自觉地排成整齐的队伍，彼此之间保持差不多相等的距离，依次前进，犹如一支步调一致的“仪仗队”。据英国《每日邮报》2016 年 11 月 16 日报道，近日，维也纳兽医学院和牛津大学的研究人员公开了一则视频，记录了鹦鹉自己取材制作工具来获取食物的过程。研究人员为四只凤头鹦鹉准备了一根它们熟悉的落叶松木枝；其他为不熟悉物品，如多叶的榉树枝，硬纸板和蜂蜡。鹦鹉的挑战是：制作出一根至少 6 厘米长的细树枝，来获取超出自己范围的腰果。研究人员在观察过程中，惊奇地发现，鹦鹉没有使用蜂蜡，而是选择撕扯

大块的树枝，然后修剪树枝，使其长度刚刚能获取屏障后面的食物。同时，它们还用鸟喙裁剪出大小适合的纸板。这一研究成果被发表在皇家学会《生物学快报》上。

人类在保护动物的同时，也充分发掘了动物的各种服务功能，使动物为人们做了大量的工作。在美国海军中，最先进的探雷队伍是海豚。美国空军军械处一等兵迪伊·詹宁斯说："它们的搜索速度快得令人难以置信。探测准确率达到100%。它们能找到任何东西。"在泰国，每年的11月10日是象节。这一天，大象被主人冲洗得干干净净，然后披红挂绿装饰一番，赶往曼谷以东425公里的素攀市，参加一年一度的"大象运动会"。比赛项目有拔河、障碍赛跑、举重、踢球以及一边跑一边拾取散落的物品等，别有一番情趣。据印度尼西亚安塔拉通讯社报道，苏门答腊南部的楠榜省政府曾制定一项训练野象耕田的计划。由于外省移民增多，原野象栖息的土地不断被开垦，出现人象争地现象，野象经常破坏庄稼。根据制定的这项计划，他们捕捉了五头野象，然后将它们送到一所训象学校，训练它们耕田。更为有趣的是，在美国加利福尼亚州有一个名叫森诺尔的小镇，"镇长"竟是一只32公斤重的黑色猎狗。有趣的是，这只名叫博斯科的猎狗是被镇上居民选为镇长的。看到这些精彩的现象，难道我们还会以为，动物世界的文明仍是周而复始和停滞不前的吗？

Civilization is the crystallization of wisdom. It is often concerned as an advanced state of human society, which only belongs to man. However, according to long-term research and investigation of biologists, many animals, as well as human, as a state of living beings, can create their own civilization in unique ways. In the book *Into Africa* , a French journalist wrote, "the most special trip is to see the same place in others' eyes. However, it is only through the eyes of animals, can we see a glimpse of goodness in man's world, aside from all the fake things."

Although animal's civilization is lower than that of man's, many of them can still produce tools and use languages, or even become musicians or language masters. Meanwhile, in their group lives, there are many signs of civilization sharing the merits of human constructions of civilization. Crabs have a sense of "unity". They often get together as groups. The crabs that already have full shell often guard outside of their caves to protect the ones that are developing new shell. A kind of honey-ant in African dessert has the spirit of "sharing". They drink honey from food, store it in their stomach, and share all of it with the empty-bellied ones, regardless of how much is left for their own. Lalas Mountain in Togo, Africa, is where "polite birds" live. These birds are nice and willing to help, with sharp head, round body, long tail and green feather. They often fly into villages, casting "gifts" into house windows. Their gifts can be flagrant flowers or delicious fruits. Local people will return their favor by offering beans or grains. They have a good memory. They come to their most hospitable hosts' houses most often, and neglect those who are not generous. Speaking about birds, there is a "hospitable" parrot living in the tropical jungles, who are friendly to their own kind as well as other birds. When they are having a banquet in forest, they often show their welcome by singing to invite other kinds of bird to share their food. In sea, sardines "respect the elderly and help the young". When a group of sardines move, they keep a certain order. When they march to a narrow place, they make sure that the young ones are on top and the old ones under. They pass such places with good order and certain distance between one another, like a guard of honor. 2016 Nov. 16th's *Daily Mail* told us about a video updated by Veterinary College of Vienna and Cambridge University, which

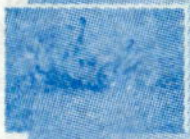

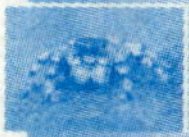

recorded the tool-making process of corellas to get food. Four corellas are offered materials like larch branches (which they are familiar of), zelkova branches with leaves, hardboard and beewax. The mission for the corellas is, to make a thin branch at least 6 centimeters long to get cashew nuts out of their reach. The researchers were surprised to find out that the corellas didn't choose beewax, but tore down a long branch and clip it to the right length to reach for the food behind a screen. The research was published on *Biology Letters* by the Royal Society.

While protecting animals, human have fully explored animals' talents, and made them do lots of work for us. The most advanced mine detection team is consisted of dolphins. "Their searching is incredibly quick, with an accuracy rate of 100%," said Dee Jennings, Lance Corporal from the Ordinance Department of America, "they can find anything." In Thailand, Nov. 10th is Elephant Festival. Elephants will be cleaned and ornamented by their owners on that day, and taken to Suphan, a city 425 kilometers to the east of Bangkok, to take part in the annul elephant Olympics. The games are tug of war, hurdle race, weight lifting, football, and picking things up when running, which are all peculiar and fun to watch. According to Antara News agency in Indonesia, a program to train wild elephants to sow was once made by local government of Lampung, an Indonesia province in south Sumatra. At that time, increasing migrants from other provinces had reclaimed the land where wild elephants lived, and crops were destroyed by those elephants when fighting with people over the land. According to the plan, the government caught five wild elephants, and sent them to an elephant training school to learn how to sow. Here is another interesting story: a town called Senault in California, US, has a 32-kilogram black hound as its town mayor. The hound named Bosco, was, surprisingly, elected by the town people. After seeing all these marvelous behaviors, no one would still mistake animals' society as a simple cycle without progress.

韦 诚 李益芳

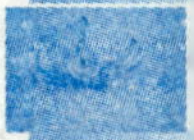

目 录

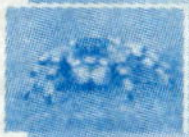

一

动物音乐家

Stories about Animal Musicians

音乐家——:英国商店雌鹦鹉,喜唱帕瓦罗蒂曲

英国西南部佩因顿城的一家宠物商店里,有一只八岁的非洲雌性鹦鹉波利,它是歌剧的忠实"发烧友"。不论白天还是黑夜,它总喜欢用口哨的方式吹着普西尼的咏叹调。特别爱扯着尖嗓门,高唱世界歌剧之王、意大利著名男高音歌唱家帕瓦罗蒂喜爱的《我的太阳》一曲,饲养过波利的盖伊先生说,他过去常常给波利播放各种古典名曲,但不知为何,当 1990 年英国广播公司 BBC 把《我的太阳》一曲作为报道在意大利举行的世界杯足球赛的主题曲时,波利对此曲情有独钟。由于广播电视不停地播放,它很快便能自己演唱。

"PARROT PAVAROTTI" IN PETSHOP

An eight-year-old female African parrot, Polly, living in a petshop in Painton, a city in the southwest of the Great Britain, is a big fan of opera. It whistles Pressigny's arias day and night, and sings *O Sole Mio* loudly, by the king of opera, world-famous high-pitched singer Luciano Pavarotti. Mr. Gay, former owner of Polly's, said, he used to play all kinds of classic songs for Polly, yet Polly was especially in favor of the song *O Sole Mio*, when it was made the theme song of 1990

World Cup by BBC. Polly learned to perform it very soon, after it was broadcast over and over again in TV and radio.

音乐家二：能歌善舞百灵鸟，革命歌曲最拿手

每天清晨，石油地球物理勘探局驻河北省某基地的宿舍区，布谷鸟、鹦鹉、喜鹊的叫声清脆悦耳，此起彼伏，就好像置身于山林野外，令人心舒气畅。

原来，这里有个叫张满林的职工，他饲养的一只百灵鸟在欢快的鸣叫。这只百灵鸟活泼可爱，不仅可以模仿十余种鸟儿的鸣叫，还能模仿人吹口哨，唱《三大纪律八项注意》，该歌曲已成了这只百灵鸟登台演出的保留曲目。每当它演奏歌曲时，又蹦又跳，可带劲了。

VERSATILE LARK SPECIALIZES IN REVOLUTIONARY SONGS

Every morning, the dormitory area of the Petroleum Geophysical Exploration Bureau in Hebei Province, China, echos the pleasant singing of cuckoos, parrots and magpies, as if it is in a mountain or a forest.

A lark is also singing happily. It is kept by a worker here named Zhang Manlin. The vibrant and lovely bird can imitate the chirp of more than ten other kinds of bird, as well as sing the song *Three Principals and Eight Notices* in whistling tone. The song is a repertoire of its own show. When singing, it also dances with full vigor.

音乐家三：大树发出音乐声，原是老鹰在享受

在非洲的一个村落，一棵华盖如云的大树里常常飘出美妙的音乐旋律。一名男青年百思不解，于是找来云梯，爬上二十多米高的大树察看。结果发现一个鹰巢，里面放有一台收音机，一只猎鹰正闭着目、点着头，陶醉在音乐的节拍中。这台收音机原来是猎鹰趁人不注意，从牧羊人那里“偷”来的。

FALCON ENJOYING MUSIC IN A TREE

A great tree in an African village often gives out beautiful melodies. A young man couldn't figure out the reason, so he found a scaling ladder, and climbed up the 20-meter-tall tree to see what was going on. He found out there was a falcon nest in the tree, with a radio in it. A falcon was reveling in the music with its eyes closed and head nodding. According to further investigation, the radio was stolen from a careless shepherd.

音乐家四：不耐寂寞热带鱼，余音绕梁大合唱

天津市一位许姓居民的家中，用鱼缸养了几十条名叫“孔雀”的热带鱼，不知什么原因，这几十条热带鱼经常吱吱地叫，闹得全家人不知所措。

一天晚上，这些热带鱼又叫起来，为此，他打电话约了几个人来家中听。人们听到这些蓝尾巴的“孔雀”吱吱叫的声音。原来，这些热带鱼正在举行“音乐会”。

CANTATA OF TROPICAL FISH

A resident named Xu in Hongxing Road, Minquan Gate, Hebei District in Tianjin City, China, raises a few dozens of a kind of tropical fish named "peacock". Their constant squeak sometimes confuses their owner.

One evening, the squeak began. Xu telephoned a few of his friends to come to his house and listen to the peculiar noise. At last people found out that it was a "concert" performed by the fish.

音乐家五：竹海琴蛙生蜀南，奇绝天下音乐会

在四川省宜宾市东南68公里处的蜀南竹海，生长着一种世间极为稀有的蛙类，它是竹蛙的一种，名叫竹海琴

蛙。琴蛙比普通青蛙略大，皮呈黄褐色，鸣声“咚咚”，如奏木琴。琴蛙因其性别年龄各异，鸣声也有高、低、缓、急之分。幼蛙，叫声娇嫩短促；老蛙，叫声低沉悠扬；雌蛙，叫声清脆；雄蛙，叫声浑厚。

每当春末夏初的夜晚，它们成群结队聚在涧谷潭畔，先是一只雄蛙挺着肚子“咚咚咚”起唱。接着，群蛙鼓着腮帮“嘣嘣嘣”地演唱起来，活像一曲木琴交响乐。这就是号称“蜀南一绝”的琴蛙音乐会。

SOUTHERN SICHUAN BAMBOO FROGS GIVING MARVELOUS CONCERTS

In Shunan *Zhuhai* (sea of bamboo in southern Sichuan), a place 68 kilometers to the southeast of Yibin City, Sichuan Province, lives a rare kind of bamboo frog named Zhuhai xylophone frog. They are a little bigger than regular frogs, with yellow and brown skin, and "dong-dong" croak like xylophone. Their croaks vary according to their genders and ages. Young frogs' croak is short and tender; old ones, long and melodious; females, clear; males, low and vigorous.

In nights of early summer, they get together near ponds or rivers. At first a male frog begins by a "dong-dong" sound, and then all the others start singing too. Their "cantata" is like a symphony of xylophones, which is taken as one of the wonders of Southern Sichuan.

音乐家六：擅长鸣叫数牛蛙，歌声回荡数公里

漫步在美洲的田原，就会听到一种类似公牛的叫声，原来它是雄牛蛙高亢的叫声。由于牛蛙的声音最远可传到两三公里以外，所以，人们又称牛蛙为"喧蛙"。牛蛙的发声器是长在嗓门里的一对黏膜褶襞，也叫声带。它那圆鼓鼓的大肚子里头还有一个气囊能起共鸣作用。当它瞪着眼睛，鼓着腮帮子唱起来时，歌声通过气囊的共鸣变得格外洪亮，几百米外都能听到"呱呱呱"的和声。

BULLFROGS SINGING ECHOS FAR

Walking on the farmlands of South America, you will hear a sound like the moo of cow. It is actually from male bullfrogs. The sound can travel to 2-3 kilometers far, so these bullfrogs are also called"loud frogs". Their vocal apparatus is a pair of mucus membrane rivel, i. e. , vocal cord. Also there is a gasbag in its big round belly, to create resonance. When the frog opens its eyes and heaves its cheek to sing, the resonance made the sound louder. Their chorus can be heard hundreds of meters away.

音乐家七:神奇八哥本领多,会念古诗会唱歌

福州市杨女士家有一只聪明的八哥叫"玛丽亚"。这只鸟会说普通话、福州话和英语,很愿意和人对话。玛丽亚念起唐诗:"春眠不觉晓,处处闻啼鸟。夜来风雨声,花落知多少。"这首诗它不但能一口气背完,而且杨女士说上句,它还能接下句。玛丽亚还喜欢唱歌。杨女士唱:"东方红",玛丽亚接唱:"太阳升。"

WONDER MYNA SINGS AND CHANTS

A clever myna named "Maria" lived with its owner, Mrs. Yang from Fuzhou. The bird could talk in Mandarin, Fuzhou dialect, and English. It liked to talk with people. Maria chants the traditional Chinese poem, "Enjoying a sound sleep in spring, everywhere the birds sing. Rainy and windy at night, countless are the fallen petals." It could not only recite the poem, but also say the following sentence after Mrs. Yang started. Maria also liked to sing. After Mrs. Yang sang, "Red in east", it followed, "The sun rises."

音乐家八：俄罗斯爵士乐队，黑猩猩风格独特

俄罗斯驯兽家伊凡诺夫领导的黑猩猩爵士乐队，不仅拥有爵士乐队不可少的定音鼓、沙球、铜鼓等打击乐，并且还有吉他、大提琴、铜管、木管、电子琴等乐器，能够演奏出很多世界著名的爵士乐曲。伊凡诺夫训练猩猩已有二十多年，这支调皮淘气的爵士乐队经过特别演奏训练，利用现代化的录音和扩音设备，演奏出的一支支爵士

乐曲韵味十足、风格独特。

UNIQUE RUSSIAN GORILLA JAZZ BAND

Russian beast training master Ivanov leads a band of gorilla, with not only percussion such as timpani, maraca and bronze drum, but also instruments such as guitar, violin, copper pipe, wooden pipe, and electronic keyboard. They can play lots of world-renowned jazz music. Ivanov has been training gorillas for more than 20 years. By his special training, the naughty gorillas can play their jazz music in their unique style with modern recording and amplifying equipment.

音乐家九：跳舞上瘾小毛驴，边走边扭险肇事

在怀远县唐集有位姓韦的唢呐爱好者，遇有重大节日，还有村里的红白喜事，他常随乐队伴奏。无事在家或田间干活休息时，他也要吹上两支曲子。他家的一头小毛驴是在唢呐声中长大的。

一次，韦某在地里耕了一会地，坐下来休息，顺手拿起唢呐吹了起来，吹着吹着，忽然发现小毛驴停止吃草，不停地摇头摆尾扭身躯。他有意停了一下吹奏，只见小毛驴也停止了扭动，开始低头吃草。只要他继续吹奏，小毛驴又会不停摆动。还有一次，主人在室内吹唢呐，家里

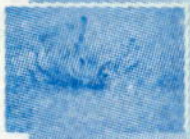

人看到小毛驴在院中又蹦又跳，很有节奏，这才知道小毛驴有“艺术细胞”。可是这头小毛驴扭秧歌不注意时间、地点和场合，有时会造成安全隐患。有一天，韦某赶着驴车去县城，走在车辆穿梭的禹王路上，他掏出唢呐吹了几下，这小毛驴边走边扭险些撞到汽车，吓得韦某赶紧放下唢呐。

DANCE-DANCE DONKEY'S DANGER

A man named Wei, living in Tang Village of Huaiyuan Town in Anhui, is a suona horn lover. On every festival or other big events, like wedding or funeral, he always plays with the local band. When he is idle at home, or having a rest after farm work, he

plays one or two pieces of music. One of his livestock, a little donkey, grew up in his suona horn sound.

One day, when Wei was having a rest after ploughing the field, he began playing the suona horn. While playing he suddenly found that the little donkey had stopped eating and started wiggling its body. When he stopped playing on purpose, the donkey started eating again. Whenever he started again, the donkey would start "dancing" again. Then the whole family found out the dancing talent in the donkey. However, its dance sometimes cause danger for it dances regardless of time or place. One day, Wei was on Yuwang Road to the town. The donkey almost hit a car when it wiggled its body while walking, after Wei began playing the suona horn. Frightened, Wei stopped playing immediately.

音乐家十：街心花园奏吉他，百鸟飞来齐欣赏

澳大利亚的吉他演奏家亨利·克温是一位杰出的艺术天才。可惜，克温的知音很少。每当他到街心花园和公园举办吉他演出时，观看的人总是寥寥无几，这种情形常使这位音乐家扫兴而归。不过，一个奇特的现象引起

了他的注意。每逢他弹奏琴弦，引吭高歌，数不清的小鸟就会从四面八方飞来，做他忠实的听众。

BIRDS ENJOYING GUITAR IN PARK

Henry Kevin was an excellent guitar artist in Australia. However, he had very few people who enjoyed him. When he performed with guitar in center parks, very few people came to see his show. He always came back disappointed. Yet he noticed that something unique happened. When he opened his voice to sing, playing the guitar, many birds would fly from all directions to be his faithful listeners.

音乐家十一：水中忽闻歌声起，演奏歌手银牙鱼

在斯里兰卡东海岸有个美丽的巴提卡洛河小港，每当夜深人静时候，人们可以随渔船在港上倾听鱼的歌声。你只要把竹竿的一端放入水中，另一端接触耳朵，就能听到远处传来美妙的“音乐”，其声时高时低，犹如人的鼻音表演。有人从船上跳入水中，潜闻鱼歌，其声就会变得像一个管弦乐队在演奏，韵律颤抖柔和。

古希腊史诗《奥德赛》中迷人的“海妖之歌”，据说描述的就是这种银牙鱼发出的演奏之音。

SILVER-FANG FISH SINGING UNDER SEA

When night falls on Batticaloa, a beautiful little port in Sri Lanka, people can enjoy fish singing on fish-boats. You can stick one top of a bamboo pole into the water, and move your ear to the other, to hear the beautiful "music" from afar, sometimes high and sometimes low, like people humming. If someone jumps into the river to hear the fish, it will sound like an orchestra, with shivering and soft melody.

The charming Song of Siren in *Odyssey*, the ancient Greek epic, is said to be the performance of this kind of fish.

点评：

鸟儿的发声器叫“鸣管”，也是长在喉咙里头。鸣管里有像薄膜一样的韧带，当它们啼叫的时候，气流通过鸣管振动韧带，歌儿就唱出来了。一些动物发出的声音不仅能使人产生愉快感，而且它们也使用和人类一样的音乐语言来创作音乐。据观察，大多数鸟都能唱1—5首歌，但反舌鸟却能唱150—250首不同的歌。它们的歌声往往是表达思想的桥梁，交流感情的需要。我们也看到，许多动物还有演奏和舞蹈天赋。

Birds give voice through an organ named “syrinx”, in their throats. There is a thin film in the syrinx. When they sing, air flows through syrinx and vibrates the film to give the sound. Therefore, animals also have brilliant music talent! Animals can not only give pleasing sounds, but also create music using music language. According to observation, most birds can sing 1～5 songs, and the shed bird can sing as many as 150～250 songs. Their songs carry their thoughts and emotions. And there are also animals with instrumental and dancing talents.

二

动物语言家

Stories about Animal Linguists

语言家一：悉尼鹦鹉语言家，专教孩子矫发音

悉尼有一所“鹦鹉语言学校”，学校里的鹦鹉不但会清楚发音吐字，而且还能掌握一些难读的、复杂的单词。这样，经过训练的鹦鹉，就从一只可爱的会说话的小鸟变成了语言矫正专家。当它们来到语音发得不准或不会念复杂单词的那些孩子们的家里时，就能帮助他们克服发音的缺陷。

SYDNEY PARROT CORRECTING CHILDREN'S PRONUNCIATION

There is a parrot language school in Sydney; parrots in the school can not only pronounce words clearly, but also manage to read very difficult words. Trained parrots are no more just lovely talking birds. They turn to a pronunciation correcting master. They can come to the homes of children with bad pronunciation or trouble spelling difficult word, and help them learn the words and how to pronounce.

语言家二：聪明喜鹊说人话，调皮捣蛋藏钥匙

北京通州区马驹桥辛屯的陈某家的孩子从树上掏了

两只小喜鹊，一只在喂养过程中死去，另一只活了下来，这只喜鹊非常能吃，鱼肉粮食无所不吃。在陈家生活的数年里，这只黑灰色的喜鹊只是偶尔飞向屋檐，从不飞走。如果有别的喜鹊来到陈家，它就会悄悄藏起来，等飞走后它又会钻出来。一天，这只喜鹊居然口吐人言，仔细分辨才明白它发出“妈”的声音，后来会说“打你”，偶尔还会学狗叫。有一次，这只调皮的喜鹊竟偷偷把门的钥匙藏了起来。后在小孩的“威吓”下，才把钥匙从草堆中扒拉出来。

CLEVER NAUGHTY MAGPIE TALKS LIKE HUMAN

In Tongzhou District of Beijing, Mr. Chen's child caught two magpies from a tree. Only one of the birds survived, which had a good appetite, eating fish, meat and grains. In the years it lived in Chen's house, the black-gray magpie never tried to fly away, only flied to the roof once in a while. When other magpies came, it hid somewhere, and only came out after the other birds flew away. One day it started talking. It said "mama" first, and then "I'll beat you", sometimes even "bark" like a dog. The other day the naughty magpie even hid the door key, and only pulled it out after "threatened" by the child.

语言家三:水族馆中一海豹,自学语言招游客

美国一妇女捡到一只小海豹,把它养在小帐篷里。它很快就学会了用鼻子开铁丝网的门,随心所欲地出入帐篷。有一次,小海豹到外面去,主人找它,小海豹竟说:"喂,你好吗?"这只海豹现在波士顿新英格兰水族馆中。每当游客来此,它会热情地说:"您好!"大声招呼"快下水池游泳吧!"

SEAL GREETS VISITORS WITH HUMAN LANGUAGE

A seal was found by an American woman, and raised in a little tent. It soon learned how to open the tent door by its nose, and then was free to be in or out. One day when it was found out of the tent, it said, "Hello! How are you?" Now it lives in New England

Sea World in Boston, when visitors come, it greets them politely, "Hello! Be quick, come here and swim!"

语言家四:狼的语言有讲究,撕咬颈项示尊敬

狼的最大特点是集群化。由于狼群觅食的范围相当广,距离较远,为此,狼嚎就成为狼群召集在一起的重要手段。其实狼的发音很复杂,除了狼嚎,还有狼吠、狼啸、狼哭、狼哀、狼鸣、狼呜、狼呻等等。每只狼的叫声都是各具特色的,因而它们很容易分辨出彼此的声音。在狼群中,撕咬颈项是表示尊敬。狼的嚎叫声调有高低之分,构成不同的联络信号,以此与正在进行捕猎的同伴保持联系。狼群中的某些成员发出嚎叫很可能是因为受到其他狼的欺负。远离的狼也用嚎叫来告诉同伴,自己在哪里。狼还往往用嚎叫声显示集体的威力。它们常常聚集在一起,像举行歌咏晚会一般地嚎叫。

WOLVES SHOW RESPECT WITH NECK-BITING

Wolves are best known for living in cluster. They often forage in faraway places, so they call each other, mostly by howling. Their voicing is complicated: howling, barking, yelling, crying, weeping, yapping, moaning, and groaning. Every wolf's voice is characterized, so they can tell each other easily. Biting

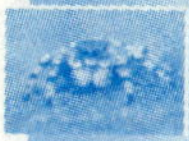

neck shows respect for wolves. They use high and low yellings to give different signals to contact with the hunting fellows. Howlings might indicate some wolves are bullied by others. Wolves far away from its cluster also use howlings to help the others locate themselves. Howling can show power to other clusters. Wolves often howl together at night, like a singing contest.

语言家五:狗说人话不稀奇,会说英语能回话

一对波兰夫妇养了一条会说英语的狗。这条名叫“霍默”的狗,智力不凡,模仿能力很强。它能用英语讲“我是霍默!”“早安!”等简单的话。

在英国伦敦，有位小姐养的一只法国小长卷毛狗却能代主人回话。一个星期天的早晨，一位洗衣工轻轻地敲门道："小姐，要洗衣吗？"那位小姐没听到，而睡在她身边的小狗却回答说："洗衣！"小狗的声音惊醒了主人，她便起身开了门。

DOGS TALK AND REPLY IN ENGLISH

A Polish couple raised a dog who could "speak" English. The dog named "Homer" is very intelligent, it could imitate human language, and say "Hello" and "Good morning" in English.

In London, a lady raised a French poodle who could make replies for its owner. A Sunday morning, a laundry man knocked gently at the door and asked, "Do you want laundry, lady?" The lady was asleep and didn't hear his words, yet the dog on her side replied, " Do the laundry!" The dog woke up its owner, and she opened the door. The laundryman told the lady about what the dog had said.

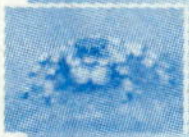

语言家六：民主德国有奇鹅，清晰呼唤主人名

德国人彼得曾得到一对日本鹅。后来，雌鹅死去，雄鹅就常与主人在家为伴，并随主人上街散步。有一次，彼

得带着雄鹅一起上街购买日用品，雄鹅看到有个小偷，乘商场人多拥挤，将手伸入彼得的裤子口袋，它用清晰的声音呼唤主人："彼得！彼得！"吓走了小偷。

GOOSE KNOWS HOW TO CALL ITS OWNER

Peter, who lived in Germany, once got a couple of Japanese geese. After the death of the female goose, the male goose accompanied its owner every day, and went to take a walk with him often. One day when Peter was shopping with it, the goose found a thief shoving his hand into Peter's pocket in the crowded shopping-mall. It yelled loudly, in clear "voice", "Peter! Peter!" The thief was scared and ran away.

语言家七：鹦鹉恶骂黄发人，军官受侮愤解雇

一只在英国海军中服役的绿色鹦鹉，不知什么原因，忽然很不喜欢棕黄色头发的人。每当看见这些人，鹦鹉就开口骂他们。许多受侮辱的士兵都原谅了这只鹦鹉。但是当鹦鹉骂一位棕黄色头发的高级军官时，激怒了这名军官，终于将鹦鹉给解雇了。

PARROT WAS FIRED FOR CURSING YELLOW-HAIRED PEOPLE

A green parrot serving in English Navy, for some reason unknown, began to hate yellow-haired people one day. It said dirty words to them once seeing these people. Many "insulted" soldiers pardoned the bird, but one commander got angry at it, and fired it for the swear words.

语言家八：训练海豚讲人话，充当水下管理员

有些科学家已经能和海豚进行交谈。事实上，有些研究者已经使海豚迅速地掌握了由十二个字母组成的话；同时，它们能够理解一些简单的短语，如"拿球来""打铃"等。

在许多国家的海军基地，一些经过训练的海豚，已经能够带着仪器进行军事侦察，为潜水员传递工具，打捞沉在海底的火箭部件，充当水下潜水员之间及海底与潜水作业人员间的往返联络员，以及在大海里管理人工养殖的鱼群。

HUMAN-LANGUAGE-SPEAKING DOLPHIN AS UNDERWATER MANAGER

Some scientists have made it possible to talk to dolphins. In fact, some researchers have taught dolphins sentences of less than 20 alphabets, and to understand simple language, like "get the ball", and "ring the bell", to name a few.

In navy bases of many countries, some trained

dolphins can perform detection with equipment, pass tools for divers, pick up rocket parts in deep sea, contact the divers, and help manage fish raised undersea.

语言家九:已届二十老雄猫,喜欢与人说说话

莫斯科有一只老雄猫,竟然能说人话,甚至可以与人作简单交谈。这只20岁老猫的主人是伊凡诺娃女士。据她说,猫是在十年前开始懂人话的,自此以后,能说的字句越来越多,至今大概可以说一百个字眼。它最喜欢说的字句包括:"我想吃东西""谢谢你"以及"我想去散步"等。猫离开所住的房间,一定会对主人说:"再见!"甚至,当它看某一个电视节目感到厌倦时,会说:"转台吧!"

TWENTY-YEAR-OLD CAT LIKES TO CHAT WITH PEOPLE

An old male cat in Moscow can talk human language, and even have simple conversations with people. The 20-year-old cat is raised by Mrs. Ivnov. She said that the cat started "talking" ten years ago, and learned up to 100 words since then. Its favorite words are, "I'm hungry" "Thanks" and "I want to go for a walk". When leaving the room, it would always say to

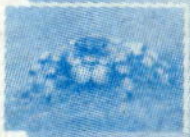

its owner, "Goodbye!" The cat would even say "please switch the channel" when the TV channel bored it.

语言家十:人类发明文字前,蝶翼已有字和数

美国华盛顿有一位大自然摄影家桑维德,他走遍 30 个国家,花费了整整 10 年时间,收集到了一套翅膀上写有 26 个字母以及由 0 至 9 数目字的蝴蝶标本。这表明,早在人类发明文字以前,神奇的大自然已在蝴蝶翅膀上写下了这些字母和数字。

BUTTERFLIES WINGS RECORDED NUMBERS AND WORDS LONG BEFORE HUMAN DID

A natural photographer from Washington collected a set of butterflies with alphabets A-Z and numbers 0-10 on their wings. He traveled to more than 30 countries in 10 years for this. This showed that long before man created language, the numbers and alphabets had been magically "written" on the butterfly winds.

语言家十一：台安有只小鹩哥，伶牙俐齿背唐诗

辽宁省台安县一位退休教师驯养了一只鹩哥能流利的背诵唐诗。小鸟身长26厘米，长着尖尖的红嘴，通身闪着黑蓝色光泽。这只鹩哥能完整背诵出"白日依山尽，黄河入海流，欲穷千里目，更上一层楼"。平日里，鹩哥除了背诗学话，有时还哼上几句从电视里听到的流行歌曲。

HILL MYNA RECITES TANG-DYNASTY POEM

In Tai'an County, Liaoning Province, a hill myna could recite poems of Tang-dynasty smoothly. Its length was 26 meters, with long, red and sharp beak, feather with black and blue gloss. It could recite the poem, "The white sun falls over the mountains, the Yellow River flows into the sea. Exhausting my eyes to a thousand *li* further, I am ascending one more story of the tower." Besides poems, the myna sometimes sang pop songs that it learned from TV, too.

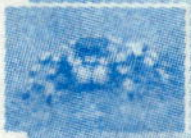

语言家十二:静谧草原卡车响,非洲大象模仿声

非洲肯尼亚的察沃草原沐浴在红彤彤的晚霞里,一望无际,美丽而静谧。一条穿越大草原的路向远远的天边延伸。一只十岁的母象还未从失去父母的阴影中摆脱出来,正同四只孤儿象徘徊在离公路约三公里的地方。可能它们有着共同的悲伤,为了排解心中的孤独和郁闷,日复一日地在红日落下的几个小时,扬起大象鼻,发出类似卡车的声音,久久地回荡在寥廓的原野。伍兹霍尔海洋研究所的科学家认为,“这一发现是人们在陆地非灵长类哺乳动物中首次发现声音模仿的本领。”

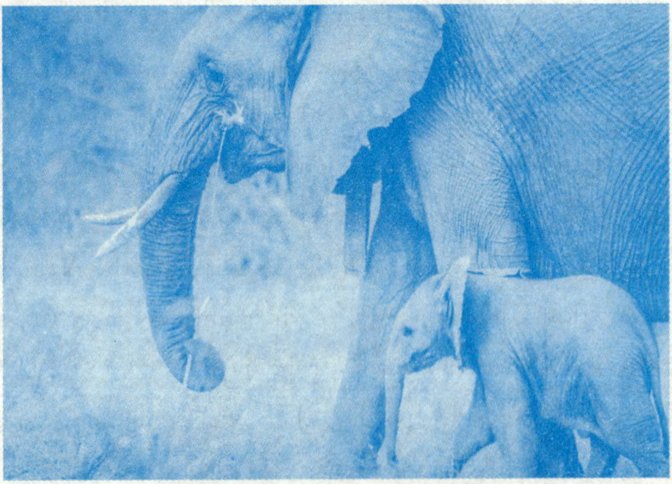

AFRICAN ELEPHANTS MIMIC TRUCK SOUND

Tsova Prairie in Kenya Africa is bathing in red sinking sun, boundless, beautiful and silent. A road stretches to the horizon through the prairie. A ten-year-old female elephant was still in the shadow of losing its parents. It strayed in a place 3 miles from the road together with 4 other orphaned elephants. They might share the same sorrow, and gave out sound like truck together in the next a few hours after sunset every day, to let their feelings out. The sound echoed in the large prairie. A scientist from Woods Hole Research Center said, "the discovery of such sound is the first example of non-primate land animals giving mimicking sounds."

点评:

语言是人们表达和交流的工具,是人区别于其他动物的本质特征之一。很多现象都表明,动物为了表达它们的喜悦和愤怒,传递它们的生活经验,以及觅食、御敌、求偶等的需要,也创造了它们特有的语言。据鸟类学家研究,乌鸦的"语言"大约就有三百多种。乌鸦为了集合伙伴,就会发出空乏失神的叫声。同时,各种动物同人类一样,由于居住地域自然条件的不同,也会产生各种各样的方言土语。譬如,美国密西根湖畔的乌鸦和意大利佛

罗伦萨的乌鸦就没有共同的语言，谁也不懂谁的“话”。当然，到目前为止，尚未发现动物为了更便捷地使用语言而发明的文字。

Language is a tool for human communication, and a distinction of human from other animals. Many signs have shown that animals have their languages, too, to pass down their life experience, and for other needs like preying, fighting and mating. According to some ornithologists, crows have more than 300 languages. To gather their friends, they give a hollow tweet. Meanwhile, just like human, animals have “dialects” according to their living environments. For example, crows living near Michigan Lake have totally different dialect from that of crows in Florence, they cannot “understand” each other. Anyway, until now, there is no proof of words invented by animals for more convenient use.

三 动物建筑师

Stories about Animal Architects

纪事一：白蚁别墅有讲究，高大雄伟保恒温

白蚁遍布于除南极洲外的六大洲，其主要分布在以赤道为中心，南、北纬度45°之间。全世界已知白蚁种类有3000余种。白蚁的巢群中一般只有一对原始型蚁王和蚁后，某些种类也有出现多王多后的现象。一旦原始型蚁王、蚁后体弱病死后，巢群内会迅速产生新的蚁王、蚁后，继续延续巢群的繁殖后代，扩展群体的需要。白蚁在巢穴门前派有卫兵执勤，凡是外来者，一律格杀勿论。

白蚁建住宅时，一边准备材料，一边施工，把所有碰到的东西一个一个堆积起来，这样，层层叠叠，盖到高达几米甚至几十米，加上它们把房子盖在高坡上，更显得壮观。白蚁的建筑工程极其繁琐复杂，整个白蚁城堡都是由唾液、泥土和粪便的混合物建成，而且所有材料都需要在它的嘴里进行调和。这种混合物像混凝土一般坚固。它们的“别墅”有空调系统，可以保持恒温，调节湿度。白蚁所建的建筑物能保持100年之久。

LARGE HOUSE OF CONSTANT-TEMPERATURE FOR TERMITES

Termites live in all six continents except for Antarctica. They mainly live in areas of latitude between 45 degree north, and 45 degree south. There are more than 3000 kinds of termites around the world. A nest of termites usually has only one pair of king termite and queen termite prototype. Some nests have more than one pair. Once the prototype pair of king and queen termites die, a new pair will quickly fill in, to procreate and expand the nest. At the "gate" of the nest, guarding termites will kill anyone who tries to break in.

When building the nest, the termites find materials and build them together at the same time. They fold the materials together to several meters or even tens of meters high. The nests are often built on hills, which made them more magnificent. The project is very complicated, for the "castles" are made of mud, saliva and waste, they have to blend these in their mouths. The mix is as firm as concrete. The "castle" has air-conditioning system to control temperature and humidity. It can last more than 100 years.

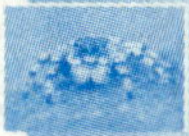

纪事二：蜜蜂造房夺天工，不愧一流建筑师

蜜蜂是当之无愧的一流建筑工程师。它们所使用的建筑材料是蜂蜡。蜜蜂靠腹节之间的腺体分泌蜂蜡，每

次分泌的蜂蜡还不及针尖大。要储存450克材料大约需要50万滴的蜂蜡。蜂巢完全用蜂蜡搭建,蜂巢内部是一排排的蜂房,非常别致精巧。

LEVEL-A ARCHITECT—BEES

Bees are born architects. They use beewax to build their houses. They produce beewax by the gland in their stomachs, each time the amount smaller than pinpoint. 450 grams of building material need 0.5 million drops of beewax. The bee nest is made only of beewax, consisting of rows of etiquette bee houses.

纪事三:软体动物鹦鹉螺,建造外壳抗压力

鹦鹉螺是一种软体动物,仅存于印度洋和太平洋海区,在中国的西沙群岛、海南岛南部地区均有发现。作为鹦鹉螺主要产地的法属新喀里多尼亚,还以鹦鹉螺作为国徽的主要图案。

鹦鹉螺生活在海面下约300米的地方。鹦鹉螺之所以能承受巨大的海洋压力,归功于鹦鹉螺靠分泌碳酸钙就能建造一个坚硬的外壳来穿越深邃的海洋。鹦鹉螺死亡后,身躯软件脱壳而沉没,外壳则漂在海上。它的名字事实上就是源自拉丁文“水手”,因为古代人们发现成群鹦鹉螺的空壳漂浮在海洋里。数学家们更专注于鹦鹉螺

外壳切面所呈现优美的螺线，螺旋中暗含了斐波拉契数列。

PEARLY NAUTILUS BUILDING SHELLS AGAINST PRESSURE

Pearly nautilus is a mollusk only in Indian Ocean and Pacific Ocean. They are found in Xisha Islands, and south of Hainan Island. New Caledonia, as the major pearly nautilus producing area, put it on its national emblem.

Pearly nautilus lives about 300 meters below sea surface. It can endure the pressure under sea, for it builds a shell by producing calcium carbonate. After its death, the soft part of the nautilus sink under sea, while the shell flows on the surface. Its name originates from "sailor" in Latin, for ancient people found many shells flow in sea. Mathematics, though, are more interested in the perfect tangent line of the shell. The shell also implies Fibonacci sequence.

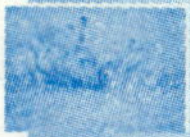

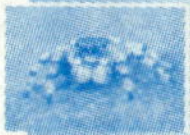

纪事四：西双版纳纺织鸟，衔草结网营巢穴

在我国云南西双版纳生活着一种会纺织的鸟。纺织鸟在营巢时，会选择一根小树枝，把硬草杆编在树枝上做

骨架。然后雄鸟和雌鸟同心协力，把软草一根根编上去，仿佛织布的模样。最后，口袋形的精致小巢便织成了。巢在顶上另有一个柄，用它悬挂在树的枝头或棕榈的叶子上。

WEAVING BIRDS IN XISHUANGBANNA BUILD NEST WITH STRAW

A weaving bird living in Xishuangbanna build their nests by adding firm grass rod on large branches. The male and female often work together to weave the grass on the branch, just like making cloth. At last a pocket-shaped little nest is built. On the nest there is often a handle to hang on tree branches or palm leaves.

点评：

动物在建筑方面历史悠久。海狸就已经有500万年建造大坝的历史。它们建造的大坝高达300米，其坚固的程度足以抵挡一辆家用汽车的冲击。动物的建造技能也是巧夺天工。蜜蜂建筑的蜂窝状房子，使同样体积的建筑，实现对空间的最充分利用。这给我们一个启示：人们要解决城市的拥挤问题，能否抛弃现在公寓楼的设计模式，而向蜜蜂学习，建造出蜂窝形建筑。如此看来，建筑学上有许多的仿生课题需要我们去研究。

Animals enjoy long history in architecture. Beavers have 5 million years history in building dams. The dams can be as tall as 300 meters, and can stand the strike of a car. Animals also have great building techniques. Bee house is a good example for a full use of space. Bees show us to a solution for crowded cities; maybe we can design buildings in their way to save space. Likewise, many other bionic researches are for us to explore.

四 动物使用工具记趣

Stories of Animals' Tool Use

记趣一：太平洋上巧乌鸦，会制倒钩和锯子

1992～1995 年，生物学家亨特在南太平洋的新喀里多尼亚岛上的雨林中从事研究工作时发现，乌鸦能制作两种截然不同的工具：一种是在一头末端带有倒钩的细枝；另一种则取材于一种边缘带有倒钩锥形的硬叶片。在制作第一种工具时，乌鸦先用自己宽大的喙从树枝中抽取一根细枝，然后使用“捏掐”的方法使细枝的末端产生明显的倒钩，以便用以抓取树洞里的幼虫。乌鸦制作的第二种工具则是以露兜树的叶子为材料，当叶子还长在树枝上时，乌鸦就在叶子边缘一口一口地连续啃咬以加深锯痕。成形后再从植物上咬下。

我们知道，乌鸦在中国往往是同不吉利相联系的。而尼泊尔每年的 8 月 10 日却是传统的“乌鸦节”。这一天清晨，尼泊尔人要将炒好的米和饼干等食物放在屋顶上和院内空地上，供乌鸦尽情“享用”，前来“过节”的乌鸦越多，主人就越高兴。

CROWS ON PACIFIC OCEAN MAKE HOOKS AND SAWS

During 1992 ～ 1995, a biologist named Hunter researching on New Caledonia, Pacific Ocean found that crows in that area could make two different tools: a barb made of branches, and a hook made of firm leaves. When making the first tool, they used their broad beaks to fetch a branch, and then pinch a hook on one end, to reach for larves inside of tree holes. The second tool was made of aggag leaves. They bit some parts of leave rim off, when the leaves were still in tree, and then bit the leaves off to use them as saws.

In China people think crows are omen signs, while in Nepal people celebrate the holiday for crows on 10th of August every year. In the early morning of the day, local people put food like cooked rice and biscuits to invite crows to their houses. The more crows come to enjoy the food, the happier the owners get.

记趣二:坦桑尼亚黑猩猩,树枝钓食白蚂蚁

英国人类学家简·古扎尔在坦桑尼亚的密林里发现,黑猩猩为了获取食物,其制作与使用工具的能力足以使人类感到震惊。

当黑猩猩发现蚁巢后,它们先将蚁巢上部的尘土小心翼翼地扒开,另外一个黑猩猩从树杈上掰下一根细长的棍子缓缓插入,并时而使劲抖几下,蚁巢里的白蚁乱成一团,纷纷涌来爬在这根细棍子上。只见执细棍子的黑

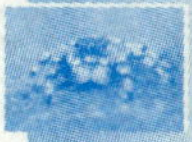

猩猩把沾满白蚁的棍子慢悠悠地抽出,随后它们轮流品尝着聚集的棍子上的白蚁,真是惬意无比!

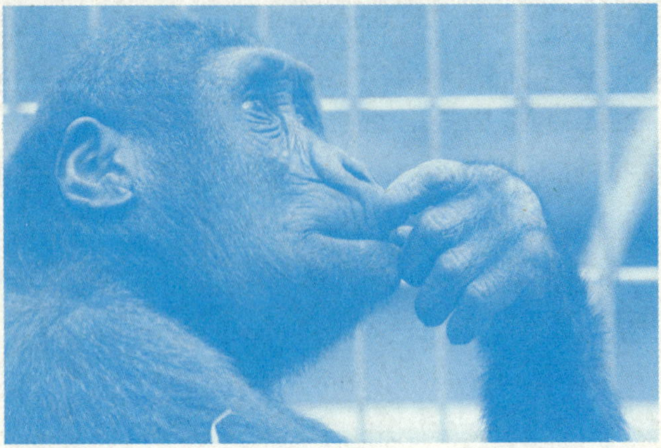

TANZANIA CHIMPANZEE USES BRANCHES TO CATCH TERMITES

Jane Gouzard, a British anthropologist found that chimpanzees have surprising talents in making and using tools to prey.

When chimps find a termite nest, one of them first carefully sweeps the dust away from it, and then another one breaks off a stick from tree branch, shoves it in the nest and stirs it with force from time to time. The termites in the nest fall into a mess, and many climb on the stick. Then the chimp takes the stick out,

and they take turns to enjoy their meal like the happiest chimps in this world.

记趣三：热带森林缝叶莺，以喙为针缝口袋

在热带森林的芒果树和番石榴树上，栖息着一种身躯娇小、尾巴很长的缝叶莺。它会把细长而微微弯曲的喙当做缝针，在脚爪的配合下，用植物的纤维、蜘蛛丝等做缝线，将树叶缝制成口袋状。为了使缝线不致松脱，它居然还会扣上结子。口袋缝好后，缝叶莺就四出寻找枯草、羽毛和植物纤维，把它们垫在里边，做成一个温暖而舒适的窝。

TAILOR BIRDS IN TROPICAL FORESTS SEW POCKETS WITH THEIR BEAKS

On Mango and Gauva trees in tropical forests, there lives a small tailor bird with long tail. It weaves plant fiber and cobweb into stitches with its beak and feet, and makes pockets with it. It even knows how to knot the stitch to keep it from falling down. Then the bird will find grass, feather and more plant fiber, to fill them in the pocket and make a warm and comfortable nest.

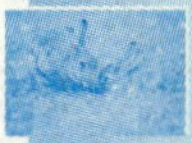

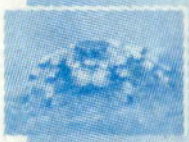

记趣四:黑海边上小鸟巢,以蛇作锁退天敌

有几位年轻人到树木茂森的黑海海边旅游,看到一个鸟巢筑在一颗高大的树上。鸟巢里的幼鸟正嗷嗷待哺。不远处的天空,一只鸟抓着一条大灰蛇,在快要飞到巢上时,却把活着的蛇放在巢门前,留下小鸟在巢里,出去觅食。原来这种鸟并不食蛇,只是将蛇脊椎弄断,作为自己住宅的"门锁"。一些野兽想闯进来,看到这把"门锁"会吓得退避三舍。

BIRD NEST NEAR BLACK SEA EQUIPPED WITH "SNAKE LOCK"

Some young people traveled to the forest near Black

Sea, and found a large nest on a tall tree with hungry birdlings. A bird flew near, with a big gray snake in its claws. It put the snake down, and went away again. The bird did not feed on the snake; it just broke the snake's spine and used it as a "lock" to scare away other beasts that wanted to come in.

记趣五:渔翁蜘蛛会钓虫,树枝作杆丝作饵

在南美洲有一种名叫渔翁的蜘蛛,它们也会抽丝,可是从来不结网,只是爬到水面附近的树枝上,吐出一根细丝粘在树枝顶端,让细丝垂下去作钓线,又在钓线下端揉成一个小团,作为"鱼饵"。然后,渔翁蜘蛛轻轻晃动树枝,让"鱼饵"酷似一只小虫。一些会飞的昆虫往往上当,

飞过来一口咬住，却被粘个正着，这时，渔翁蜘蛛马上从树枝上爬下来，慢慢享用。

FISHERMAN SPIDER FISHING WITH ROD AND COBWEB

A fisherman spider in South America never build a web, but use its silk to fish. It climbs on a tree branch near water, and produce silk stitches, with one thin end sticking on the branch and the other larger end down to the water as a fish bait. Then it waggles the branch slightly to make the bait look like a small insect. Many flying insects will often bite on it, only to be glued by the silk. Then the fisherman spider will climb down to enjoy them.

记趣六：巧使土块黄鼠狼，白赔诱饵几斤肉

四川省的农民江某等人发现田间有黄鼠狼出没，顿生捕猎念头。于是，江某等人买来猪肉煮熟，涂上小磨麻油锁入设计的“机关”，晚上布在田里。第二天一早，他们到现场一看，个个目瞪口呆，捧夹全部翻出了土，肉饵不翼而飞了。当天，他们又买了一公斤肉饵，重新将捧夹布置好，当晚伏在沟边看个究竟。午夜时分，忽见十多只黄鼠狼跑来。几只大黄鼠狼跑过去，搬来土块，两后爪着

地，两前爪捧起土块挨个将捧夹砸翻。然后它们蜂拥而上，抢食肉饵。一旁暗察的江某等人白白赔了几斤肉，还一夜没睡觉。

YELLOW WEASEL USED SOIL BLOCK TO GET MEAT FROM TRAPS

One day a villager named Jiang and his fellows found signs of yellow weasels in their fields, so they decided to catch the animals. They bought pork, boiled and oiled it, and then put it into the traps in the field. The next morning, they were shocked by what they saw: the traps were filled with soil, while the meat were all gone. They soon bought another kilo of meat to reset the traps, and hid near the field to see what happened. At midnight, suddenly about a dozen of weasels came. A few big ones destroyed the traps with some soil blocks, and then all of them scrambled for the meat. Yet for Jiang and his fellows, they lost kilos of meat, and a night's sleep.

点评：

长期以来，人们总认为地球上只有人类才会有意识地制造和使用工具。事实上，当人们了解了动物世界时，就会发现，在自然界有许多动物也同人类一样，为实现某

种愿望和目的，会制造和使用工具。它们不仅会利用天然工具来取食、御敌，而且懂得利用杠杆原理，借助树枝来撬开东西等等。当然，它们制造的工具还很难像人类制造的那样精致多样。

People often think that we are the only animal on earth that can intentionally make tools. While in fact, when we know more about animals, we will find surprisingly that they are not only capable of making and using tools to prey or defend the enemies, but also using more complicated tools such as leverage. Yet their tool-making craft is still not as good as ours.

五 动物智慧奇趣

Other Stories about Animal Wisdom

奇趣一：游弋大海鹦鹉鱼，睡觉穿衣醒来脱

在印度阿明迪维群岛以及克代夫群岛附近的大海里，栖息和繁衍着一种鹦鹉鱼。每当夜幕降临的时候，鹦鹉鱼就会分泌出一种晶莹透明的液体，将周身严严实实地包裹起来，就像穿了一件漂亮的“睡衣”。这“睡衣”坚韧如钢铁，任何海上的霸王也休想侵犯它，即使将它囫囵吞下，也要乖乖地吐出来，因为睡衣表面的物质有强烈的致呕作用。

每当凌晨来临的时候，鹦鹉鱼又分泌出另一种黏液，将美丽的睡衣溶解得一干二净，在安然歇息了一夜之后，便毫不费力地游走了。

PARROT FISH WEARS PAJAMA IN SLEEP AND TAKES IT OFF AFTER

In the sea near some Indian islands, there lives a kind of parrot fish. At night it produces a crystal-like liquid to wrap itself in, just like wearing a beautiful pajama. The “pajama” is firm as steel, no living thing in the ocean can invade it, nor swallow it, because it has a strong nauseant effect.

When the morning comes, parrot fish gives out another mucus to dissolve its “pajama”, and delightfully swims away.

奇趣二：马开汽车顶呱呱，交通规则也精通

在美国路易士维尔市的大街上，有一辆经改装的林肯牌汽车，正以时速 8 公里的速度在公路上行驶。汽车的驾驶员是一匹名叫“牛油糖”的马。这匹马站在车厢里稳健地驾驶着汽车，不仅会操纵方向盘，还会开动引擎、挂档及踩油门和刹车，尤其是在遇到行人时，它还会按喇叭，发出警告。

HORSE DRIVER

On the road of Louisville, a Lincoln car is running on the road at the speed of 8 yard. The driver is a horse named "Butterscotch", driving the car, standing. It can

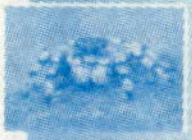

not only handle the wheel, the engine, the gears and the paddles, but also honk to warn the passengers.

奇趣三:随波逐流小海星,金蝉脱壳本领强

海星俗称"星鱼",是一种棘皮动物,体色鲜艳多彩,一般呈星状,常年栖息在海洋的浅水区。它们看上去似乎是无生命的,或随波逐流,或贴附于岩壁,或在退潮时同海草一起搁浅于海滩。

对于已经长大成年的海星来说,除了海獭、海鸥偶尔来袭击外,几乎没有什么天敌可言。海星在遇到劲敌伤害时,会施展一种特有的逃跑术。它们自行脱掉臂腕,逃之夭夭。海星具有较强的再生能力,失去的臂腕很快就会长出来,只是比原来的小一点;就是脱落的臂腕本身,也能自行长成一条完整无缺的新海星。

STARFISH ESCAPES BY LOSING LIMBS

Starfish belongs to enchinodermata, with colorful, star-shaped bodies. They live in shallow water areas of sea. They often move by tide, or attach themselves to the rocks, or strand on beach together with seaweeds, so they don't look lifelike.

For grown starfish, they don't have many enemies, just occasionally attacked by sea otters or seagulls.

They are excellent at escaping when attacked. They get rid of their own limbs, and swim away. The lost limbs will soon grow back, for starfish has strong restoring power. The lost limb itself, can grow to be another starfish, too.

奇趣四:信鸽识途本领高,寻找归途靠路熟

英国牛津大学的研究人员用了 10 年时间,通过全球定位系统对信鸽进行研究,终于破解了信鸽寻找归途的非比寻常的能力。他们发现,信鸽并不是根据太阳升落的方向飞行,而是与人一样,懂得认路。信鸽往往是沿着高速公路飞行,在交叉路口处转弯,甚至会沿着交叉路口的环岛转弯,增添了不必要的行程。

HOW PIGEONS KNOW THE WAY

A research team from Cambridge University spent 10 years on investigating pigeons with global location system, and finally knew the secret of their ability in telling the way. They found that the pigeons don't fly according to the direction of sun, but know the way just like human. They often fly in the same direction of the highway, and turn at the crossings, or even at roundabouts, which make them travel further than

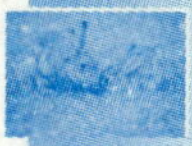

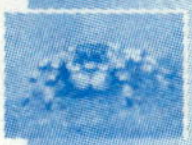

necessary.

奇趣五：阿尔卑斯山猴子，出山觅食用气功

在法意瑞边境的阿尔卑斯山上，有一种猴子，体形如野兔。这种猴子有一种特别的本领，即气功，堪称“气功高手”。每当寒冬冰雪封山，它们为了尽快出山觅食，先运好气，然后飞快地向山下滚去，不管山势如何陡峭，也伤不了一根筋骨。

MONKEYS ON ALPS USE QIGONG TO PREY

On the border of French, Italy and Germany, there is a monkey that looks like rare. They have a special "Qigong", which helps them rolling down very fast from the top of the mountain without hurt, to prey in cold winter.

奇趣六：大象酿酒寻自醉，醉后游荡丛林中

非洲大象为了享受喝饮美酒的快乐，常常为自己酿造琼浆玉液。大象把从树上掉下来的水果扒到坑里，用树叶和杂草盖上发酵，发酵完成后，就吃这种糊状物。大象喝醉后，就会像醉鬼一样在热带丛林里到处游荡。

ELEPHANTS ENJOY WINE AND WANDER IN JUNGLES DRUNK

African elephants enjoy wine very much, and they

often make their own drinks. They gather fallen fruits together in a pit, and cap them with leaves and grass for fermentation. Then they will eat the pasty and drink the wine. After getting drunk, they will wander in the tropical forest like drunkards.

奇趣七：印度有鸟会点灯，照明去捉萤火虫

在印度，有一种生活在巢穴的鸟。为了壁厚而阴暗的巢穴明亮起来，雄鸟便会飞到附近的沼泽地，从那里衔回很粘的泥土，把它粘到巢壁上，然后，又捉来萤火虫，用爪子固定在粘泥上，使它飞不走。这样，当雄鸟连捉几只，甚至几十只萤火虫后，鸟巢内就被照得非常明亮。接着，这种鸟又用同样的办法把鸟巢外部也装饰得星火点点，远远望去，整个鸟巢如同一盏闪光的灯。

INDIAN BIRDS USE GLOWWORMS AS LIGHT

In India there is a bird living in nest. For the enlightenment of its nest, the male bird will catch glowworms and pick up mud from bogs to glue them to the nest. They put the glowworms both in and out of the nest, to make it look like a light.

奇趣八：大洋洲内捕鱼猪，大海捕鱼为生计

在大洋洲的托克劳群岛上，约有300只会游泳捕鱼的猪。这群猪不知来自何方，它们到法考福岛上后，由于缺乏传统食物，被迫要适应环境，到海里捕鱼为生。这些猪都是游泳能手，它们到了海里，就像在陆地一样，上蹿下跳，捉到大鱼后，回到岛上享用。

FISHING PIG IN OCEANIA

On Tokelau islands of Oceania, there are about 300 pigs that can swim. Nobody knows where they come from, yet they were forced to adapt to the environment when they just came. Now they know how to fish, and have become excellent swimmers. They often enjoy their fish on the land.

奇趣九：人与猩猩共炒股，猩猩比人会赚钱

一家瑞典报纸给五名股市分析家每人2000美元，也给一只黑猩猩2000美元，任由他们在股票市场上买卖股票。一个月之后，黑猩猩奥拉所买的股票增值了304美元，排名最高。排名第二的分析家报买的股票只增值了208美元。

GORILLAS OUTWEIGH MEN IN STOCK MARKET

A Swedish newspaper gave 5 stock analysts and a gorilla \$2,000 each, and asked all of them to buy or sell stocks with the money at their own wishes. A month later, the stock bought by the gorilla raised \$304 in value, which was the highest. The stock of the analyst who ranked the second only raised \$208.

奇趣十：蚂蚁也会做交换，昆虫残肢换树叶

有一天，一只蚂蚁从远处运回一块风干了的昆虫残肢，这时另一只蚂蚁拖着一片很小很轻的干枯了的植物叶片也在向巢穴奔去。两只蚂蚁在半路上相遇了。运叶片的蚂蚁停了下来，两只蚂蚁相距三四厘米的距离，同时

将自己的触角摆动一会儿后便达成协议，两只蚂蚁把食物进行交换后，共同向着同一个巢穴奔去。

ANTS TRADE INSECT BODY WITH LEAVES

One day an ant carried back a dried insect part from afar, and met another one that was carrying a dried leaf to the same nest. They stopped with a distance of 3～4 centimeters, and wiggled their antennas towards each other. Then they reached some agreement, exchanged their "goods" and started their journey together towards the nest.

奇趣十一：佛罗里达一猩猩，作画可卖数千元

美国佛罗里达州一家画廊挂了两幅现代抽象画。参观者对这两幅画都给予相当高的评价。有人还对这两幅画爱不释手，一名美术交易商甚至表示，这两幅画他可以卖到数千美元的价格。其实，这是一家周刊特别为现代美术爱好者“设计”的趣味实验。他们找了一只红毛猩猩，让它用画笔、手指，甚至嘴唇作画，然后挂在画廊里，询问参观者的意见。

GORILLA PAINTER IN FLORIDA SELLS ITS PAINTINGS AT GRANDS

A gallery in Florida had two highly-valued paintings, which could be sold at thousands of dollars according to an art dealer. This was an interesting experiment designed for the modern art lovers, by a magazine. The painter was a red-haired gorilla, who was invited by the magazine to paint with pens, its fingers and or even lips.

奇趣十二：警察电话嚎叫声，原是小猪为活命

一天，美国加州维德伍德的警察突然接到一个紧急求救电话。然而当警方拿起听筒之后却听不到对方说话，只听到一阵阵猪似的嚎叫，情况紧急，警方根据查出的报警电话号码，迅速驱车赶到该市居民斯洛尔斯基家，发现打电话求救的是一头体重23公斤的小母猪。据女主人说，这头叫“维罗”的小猪是他们家养的宠物，但它近来却常和男主人过不去。每天早晨它都要闯进卧室冲着正在睡觉的男主人尖声怪叫。为此，男主人曾数次表示它要再这样就将它杀了吃。这次或许它是为了避免被杀而向警方求救。

PIG HOWLS TO CALL 911 FOR LIFE

One day the police of Wadewoods, California got a phone call from a family named Sloreski. Nothing but pig's howl came from the phone. Taking this as an emergency, the police rushed to the house, only to find the call was from the pet pig. The 23-kilo pig didn't went on well with its owner at the time. It screamed to him every morning. The owner threatened to kill it, and that was why it called for help.

奇趣十三：奥地利的小公猪，会探雷的好工兵

奥地利的一位军事教官与一名动物学家合作，经过半年的训练，终于使一头名叫“黑球”的小公猪，成为出色的“工兵”。“黑球”能嗅出埋在地下的各式地雷，并以狂吠向主人示意。一次，它在表演时，仅用一小时，就将事先埋下的100多个实验地雷一一发现。

LITTLE PIG FROM AUSTRIA, GOOD MINE HUNTING ENGINEER

A little pig named "Blackball" was trained as a mine hunting soldier by a half-year training, the cooperation of a trainer and a zoologist. It could tell all kinds of mines, and howl to its owner to inform them. On a performance it found more than 100 experimental mines in less than an hour.

奇趣十四：体小灵巧寄生蚁，专门打劫不干活

有一种体小灵巧的寄生蚂蚁，它们从不干活，而是把自已的巢营建在别的蚁巢旁边，不时地窥测附近蚁巢的动向。一旦有机可乘，便进行闪电式的掠夺，把别的蚁巢中的卵和食物抢劫一空。待别的蚂蚁闻讯赶来，它们已全部撤走，只留下一个空巢。万一别的蚂蚁穷追不舍，它们能放出一种难闻的气味，迫使追赶者止步。

SMALL PARASITIC ANT ROBBER DOING NOTHING ELSE

Akind of small and quick parasitic ant never does any work, but builds its nest near that of other ants, and watches them. At the first chance they rob all the eggs and food of the near nest. When the owners of the nest come back, they are already gone with an empty nest left. If the victims pursue them, they give out a bad smell to stop the revenge.

奇趣十五：老鼠偷运大苹果，谐趣横生齐用力

一位上海居民童某深夜回家，忽听到墙角边有细碎声响，循声细看，只见一只小老鼠四脚朝天抱着苹果，另一只大一点的老鼠则咬着小老鼠的尾巴使劲向后拖。第二天，童某在打扫卫生时，发现一只盛放书籍的纸箱内，竟有三只完好无损的苹果，其周围存满了碎纸屑及花生果壳之类过冬物品。

HOW RATS MOVE BIG APPLES TOGETHER

One day a Shanghai native Tong went home at midnight. He heard a little sound from the corner of the wall, and it was a bunch of mice stealing apples: a little mouse with an apple in its four limbs, and a bigger one pulling its tail. The second day, Tong found a paper box with three whole apples, some peanut shell, and warm-keeping objects like scraps of paper.

奇趣十六：超级老鼠智商高，懂得避开毒鼠药

据香港《大公报》载，美国政府一份秘密报告透露，一种超级老鼠已开始"占领"英国及世界一些地方。报告说，已发现一种超级聪明，智商相当于八岁儿童的超级老

鼠，它们懂得避开现在任何已知的对付老鼠的毒药。专家还指出，在世界各地均可发现这种超级老鼠的踪迹。

SUPER INTELLIGENT RATS KNOW POISON

According to *Ta Kong Pao* of Hong Kong, a secret report of American Government said that a super intelligent rat has "occupied" some parts of world. It was said that they were as clever as 8-year-old children, so clever as to tell all the known poison against rats. Experts also pointed out that they live all over the world.

奇趣十七：只因爱闻此香气，飞鼠奋勇保名药

在湖北神农架，常常会有一种飞鼠同药农斗智斗勇。当药农发现峭壁上的金钗石斛，悬绳采摘时，常常会从树林里或岩洞中突然飞出一只脸像狸，眼睛似猫，嘴巴像鼠，耳朵似兔，前爪锋利，全身的毛为棕褐色的飞鼠，扑向农药上方的绳索，并将之咬断，使药农葬身山谷。飞鼠之所以要咬断绳索致药农于死地，是因为它特别爱闻金钗石斛散发出的香气。

FLYING RATS PROTECTING HERBS FOR THE SMELL

In Shennongjia of Hebei, a kind of flying rats often fight with local herb collectors. When these collectors pick up dendrobium stems on the cliffs, some rats with palm civet's face, cat's eyes, mouse's mouth, rabbit's ears, sharp claws and brown fur, often rush out all of a sudden from woods or craves, to bite off their rope. Sometimes they would fall down the cliff after the rats' attack. The reason of this is they love the smell of dendrobium stems, and want to keep them from the collectors.

奇趣十八：母亲带队小老鼠，咬住尾巴防迷失

有一种食虫类老鼠，新生的小鼠在一周内睁不开眼睛。老鼠的母亲每天带领自己的孩子到洞外散步。它们生来总是由母亲带路，小鼠一个个咬住前面的老鼠尾巴根上的毛，排成一列纵队，以防止没睁开眼的小老鼠迷路。

MOTHER MOUSE LEADS THE WAY OF ITS BABIES

There is a kind of mouse, who cannot open its eyes in the first week of its life. Mother mouse lead its babies to take a walk every day. They walk in a line, and each of them bites into the front one's tail, so none of them would get lost.

奇趣十九：徐老汉家稀奇事，家鼠喜欢看电视

1986年的一天晚上，江苏盐城市徐老汉正在看电视，偶然发现身后碗橱顶上有一只家鼠目视荧光屏。当他招呼家人看时，家鼠立即溜之大吉。过了几天，徐老汉一家人又一次亲眼目睹了家鼠趴在橱顶上看电视。这事很快被左邻右舍传为奇闻。眼见为实，一些好奇者便前往徐家辨真伪。晚上在播放日本电视连续剧《血的迷路》时，大家静心等候这只小生灵的光顾。果然一只约十公分长的灰鼠在碗橱顶上出现了，只见它竖起耳朵，旁若无人地俯视荧屏，欣赏异国风情。

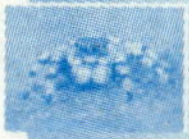

MOUSE LOVES WATCHING TV IN OLD MAN'S HOUSE

On a night in 1986, an old man named Xu was watching TV. He found a mouse staring at the TV, too. When he called upon other people, the mouse went away. Another day this happened again. The news went to his neighbors, and they became interested in the mouse. Finally, one day, after a long waiting, they found the TV loving mouse, which was enjoying a Japanese TV series on the top of the cupboard.

奇趣二十：墨西哥蚂蚁放牧，蝶形蚜虫受照顾

在墨西哥南部森林中，有一种会放牧的蚂蚁。它们能“豢养”和“放牧”一种罕见的蝶形蚜虫，以获取它们身上的分泌物。蚂蚁常常用叶子或木条把蚜虫围起来，一旦遇到蚜虫的敌人，就把它们赶走。有些蚂蚁对蚜虫的照顾可真细致周到，每到秋天时节，它们又把蚜虫搬回蚁巢中过冬，初春又把蚜虫搬回植物上去寄生，真是道道地地的“放牧者”。

MEXICAN ANTS TAKE CARE OF APHID

In southern Mexican forest, an ant can graze and raise a kind of butterfly aphid, to get their secreta. The ants encircle the aphids by leaves or branches, and drive away their enemies. They take care of the aphids with all heart, by moving them to the ant nest in autumn, and to the parasitic plants in spring.

奇趣二十一：美洲蚂蚁种菌类，分工合作防偷食

生活在美洲中部和南部的切叶蚂蚁是真正的“种植者”。它们成群结队在树林里，用剪刀状的双颚把叶子切成小片，顶在头上搬回蚁巢，乍一看好似撑着一把“伞”。叶片搬到蚁巢后，由其他工蚁咀嚼成浆状，作为培养菌类的原料。当菌类生长时，就成为蚂蚁的食料。地下蚂蚁“菌园”十分庞大，有的长 1 米、宽 0.3 米，还配有专门的警卫蚁，以防外来蚂蚁偷食。

AMERICAN ANTS RAISE FUNGUS IN UNITY AGAINST STEALING

Leafcutter ants in central and southern America are true “farmers”. They cut the leaves into small pieces in the woods, and move them back to the nest, like holding an umbrella. Ants in the nest chew the leaves into sauce to fertilize fungus. They feed on fungus. Their cultivation lands underground are huge. Some are 1 meter in length, and 0. 3 meter in width, deployed with guardian ants, to prevent stealing by other tribes.

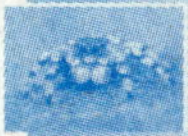

奇趣二十二:母鼠为备过冬粮,蜂窝煤堆藏山芋

一年冬天,蚌埠市民李某发现放在饭厅桌上的一个塑料菜篮中的山芋突然没有了。数天后,当家人清理蜂窝煤堆时,发现里面有三四只幼鼠受到惊吓,叽叽地叫着。定神一看,在几只幼鼠的边上堆放着那些已经干瘪的山芋。一定是母老鼠将山芋运到窝里帮助幼鼠过冬呢!

MOTHER MOUSE HID SWEET POTATO IN COAL PILE FOR WINTER

One day in 1990, Li from Bengbu found his sweet potatoes in a plastic bag missing. Some days later when they cleaned their coal pile, a few baby mice inside gave some frightened chirps. They found the missing sweet potatoes near the mice, dried. It must be the mother mouse who slipped the food in for winter.

奇趣二十三:战功赫赫牧羊犬,智勇双全建奇功

英国训练的德国牧羊犬,在 1977 年一年里就协助侦破了 14000 起案件。在埃以战争中,两国士兵的尸体都被埋在西奈沙漠里。联合国借用了 6 条英国训练的军

犬。在6周中，它们躲过坦克，避开地雷，共找到了400多具尸体。

SHEPHERD DOG WITH MILITARY GLORY

The German shepherds trained in the Great Britain, helped the detection of 14,000 cases in the year 1977 only. In the war between Egypt and Israel, corpses of the soldiers were all buried in the Dessert of Sinai. The United Nations borrowed six of them to find the bodies. In two weeks, they found more than 400 bodies despite of the attack of tanks and bombs.

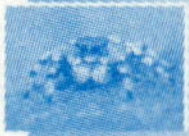

奇趣二十四：蚂蚁灭火用蚁酸，不畏牺牲战火焰

一天，法国昆虫学家法布尔为了研究蚂蚁的防火能力，把一只点燃的蜡烛放在蚂蚁窝顶上，大约一分多钟后，蚂蚁觉察到了“火警”。开始，它们惊慌失措，急急奔走，接着，好像商量好了似的，无数蚂蚁便勇敢地爬上燃烧着的烛芯，分泌出其特有的蚁酸灭火。一些蚂蚁“牺牲”后，马上又有别的蚂蚁“冲”过去。经过一分多钟的“战斗”，蜡烛火焰终于被扑灭。

ANTS USE ACETIC ACID TO FIGHT FIRE

One day, French entomologist Fabre put a lightened candle on the top of an ant nest, to see how they fight fire. After about a minute, the ant found the fire. At first they ran around in a loss, and then many ants crawled to the candle fire, and give out acetic acid to put it out. After some of them fell, others took the place of the dead ones. After a fight of more than a minute, the candle fire was finally put out.

奇趣二十五：印度班加罗尔城，狗驮猴子到处逛

在印度的班加罗尔城，每天上午大约 9 点 30 分，总

能看到一只猴子等在这里，紧接着一只狗也摇头晃脑而来。狗把猴子驮到背上，带着它到处游逛。它们天天聚会，从不失约，从不迟到。这对异族伙伴的友谊成了当地一大奇闻，招来了好多游客。

A MONKEY TRAVELS BANGLORE ON A DOG

Every day on 9:30 a. m., on a street of Banglore, people can always see a monkey waiting. Then comes a dog. The dog put the monkey on its back and take it to all the places of the city. Their cooperation happens everyday, and became one of the local legends. Lots of tourists have come to the city to witness their cross-species friendship.

奇趣二十六：北京一号注册犬，感情丰富有灵性

当北京第一次对家养犬实行注册登记制度时，因为每年都要交纳价格不菲的注册登记费，一户人家对是否继续养犬进行了争论。这个问题他们从未向小狗“玛丽小姐”说过，而恰恰在这个时期，玛丽小姐的情绪显得萎靡不振，饭也不吃，对主人也很不愿意理睬。这种情况持续了两天。直到有一天晚上，主人决定性地说：“玛丽小姐一定要养，哪怕我们的生活水平降低一些，只要我们有饭吃，就一定要遵纪守法，就一定要交纳养犬注册费！”话

刚说完，没有想到的是，玛丽小姐立刻扑到主人的怀里，眼睛里闪烁着激动的泪光，然后在屋子里欢快地转了一圈后，立刻到饭盒边吃饭去了，使在场的全家人都惊愕不已。这家人成为了北京市第一个交纳养犬注册费的人家，犬牌号码是：00000001 号。

BEIJING'S FIRST REGISTERED DOG WITH A TENDER HEART

When Beijing started registering dogs, an argument about whether to keeping the pet dog happened in a local family, for the annul registering fee was high. They never talked to their pet dog "Miss Mary" about this, while the dog seemed to be depressed at the time. It refused to eat or communicate with its owners for about two days. One night, at last, the owner said, "We must keep Miss Mary, no matter how much registering fee we need to pay. As long as we can afford, we will pay the registering fee according to the regulations." Surprisingly, after his speech, Miss Mary jumped into his arms with tears. After a happy run around the room, it went straight to its bowl and started eating. The family was the first to pay the registering fee, and Miss Mary's register number was No. 1.

奇趣二十七:骷髅天蛾会欺骗,乔装蜂王偷吃蜜

在欧洲的田野树林里,生活着一种天蛾,身上的图案极像骷髅,人称“骷髅天蛾”。骷髅天蛾最喜欢吃蜂蜜,它经常观察蜜蜂飞行的路线,尾随找到蜂房。到了蜂房门口,它就用触须摩擦吻部,发出一种类似蜂王“分娩”时发出的声音。担任门卫的工蜂听到这种声音,以为是蜂王驾到,就会恭恭敬敬地退到一边。骷髅天蛾就大摇大摆地走进蜂房,在里面暴吃一顿,然后悄悄溜走。

SKELETON SPHINX PRETENDS AS QUEEN BEE TO STEAL HONEY

In an European forest there is a sphinx with skeleton shapes on its wings, they are called "skeleton sphinx". They love honey and often follow the bees to their nests, and give out a voice like a queen bee in labor. The guard bees think the sphinx was their queen, so they step back to let it in. The sphinx will have a great meal in the nest, and then sneak away.

奇趣二十八:南美荒原植树鸟,植树造林有绝技

在南美秘鲁的一些荒野,生息繁衍着一种名叫"卡西亚"的鸟。这种鸟的头部呈白色,身上的羽毛又黑又密,长长的嘴巴十分尖利,看上去就像乌鸦。这种鸟主要靠吃一种生命力旺盛的甜柳为生。它们吃甜柳的方法极其特别,先将嫩枝咬下来,衔到荒野里,然后用嘴巴在地上挖一个小洞,把嫩枝插进去,才慢慢享用。"卡西亚"鸟啄食后的残枝虽然没了树叶,但用不了几天就能长出嫩芽,两个月左右便可长到一米左右。由于"卡西亚"鸟喜欢成群结队啄食树叶,因而等它们吃饱嫩叶飞走后,就会留下一片残枝,并很快长出成片的树林。所以,人称"植树鸟"。

PLANTING BIRDS' TALENT IN SOUTH AMERICA

In the wild lands of South America lives a bird named "Kasia". It has white head, black feather and long sharp beak, like a crow. It mainly eats a vibrant sweet wallow, in a peculiar way. They bite the tree branches off, dig a hole on the ground, shove them into the mud, and eat the leaves. Though the branch lost its leaves, it will grow new bud in a few days. In two months it can grow to 2 meters. Kasia birds often visit the wallow in group, so after they finish, many branches will be planted in the mud, and turn into new trees soon. So the bird is also called "planting bird".

奇趣二十九：鹧鸪智商实在高，骗得猎人直顿足

鹧鸪的窝通常筑在草丛中，如果有敌人走近它的窝，凭着灵敏的听觉和视觉，它会很快发现，提前展翅高飞。一天，一只雌鹧鸪正在地上孵蛋，突然发现一位猎人正向自己走来。它灵机一动，主动出现在猎人面前，一拐一瘸，蹒跚而行，猎人误以为可以轻取，就尾随追赶，不再向周围搜索。当雌鹧鸪把猎人引得远离雏群之后，突然展翅高飞，把猎人骗的目瞪口呆，顿足长叹。

SMART FRANCOLIN CHEATS THE HUNTER

Francolins build their nests in grass, so they can find out approaching enemies by its good hearing and sight and escape in advance. One day when a female francolin was brooding its eggs, it found a hunter walking towards the nest. It appeared suddenly before the hunter, pretending to be cripple, and lured him away from its children. After that, it flew away in less than a second, leaving the hunter stunned.

奇趣三十：苍鹭叼羽作诱饵，抛砖引玉捕鱼虾

在长江以南的小溪、湖泊边，常有苍鹭在浅水区轻飞慢走，一边梳理着羽毛，一边注视着水面。当胸前的白色羽毛脱落时，它就衔在喙尖，然后走下水。小鱼虾发现苍

鹭的影子,马上会躲在水草下或水深的地方。苍鹭尖锐的目光早已看得清清楚楚,它不慌不忙,在离小鱼不远的地方停住脚步,过一小会,将羽毛投进水中。这时,躲藏在水里的小鱼虾,正探头探脑地张望,以为羽毛是掉入水中的小昆虫,急忙过来抢食,早有准备的苍鹭迅速伸出长长的喙,接二连三地啄住小鱼虾。

HERON CATCHES FISH AND SHRIMPS BY FEATHER

Near the ponds and brooks south of the Yangtze River, you can often see herons walk along the water, brushing their feather and gazing at the water. When white feather comes down a heron's chest, it put the feather into its beak and goes down to water. Little fish and shrimps hide themselves under water while seeing it. The heron sees them already, and it stops not far away from them. After a while it casts the feather into water. The fish and shrimps think the feather was an insect fallen into the river, and come to eat it. The heron easily catches them one by one with its beak.

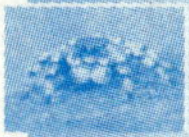

奇趣三十一:螃蟹遭遇蟹獴袭,弃足保命学壁虎

每当夜色降临,螃蟹就从池塘中爬出来,上岸逮小昆虫吃,可它最担心的是碰到蟹獴的袭击。蟹獴比家猫大

一点，是凶狠的食肉动物，当螃蟹出来吃夜餐时候，它会从暗处窜出，抓住螃蟹，这时螃蟹只能自认倒霉，丢下一只大腿，落荒而逃。当然，过不了多久，还会长出新足。

CRAB ATTACKED BY MONGOOSE GIVES UP FEET LIKE GECKO

When evening comes, crabs crawl out of ponds and prey. They are aware of the attack of crab-eating mongoose. The mongoose are a little bigger than cats. They often attack the crabs from darkness. At the moment, crabs can only give up one of its feet and run away. In a short time, the foot will grow back again.

奇趣三十二：狐狸机智戏猎人，猎人弃狗又丢鱼

一年冬天，猎人带着猎狗，驾着一辆马车去冰上捕鱼。一只狐狸被猎狗发现了，猎狗本能地去追赶狐狸。狐狸慢慢地小跑，故意把猎狗引往河中心冰薄的地方，只听"咔嚓"一声，猎狗掉入了冰窟窿。猎人费了好大劲，也未能救出猎狗，只好独自捕鱼。

在猎人驾着马车满载而归的路上，远远看见一只狐狸躺在地上，到了跟前，以为是死狐狸，就捡起来扔在马车上。他不知道狐狸是装死的。趁猎人不注意，狐狸衔起车上的鱼一条一条往下丢，然后逃之夭夭。等到猎人

到家，才发现上当。

FOX HOAXES HUNTER OUT OF HOUND AND FISH

A hunter went fishing on winter riding a carriage, with his hound. The hound found a fox and ran after it. The fox tricked the hound by leading it to an iced pond, and the found fell into the water where the ice was thin. The hunter failed to rescue his hound, and fished by himself.

When he returned with a carriage of fish, he saw the fox lying on the ground. He thought it was dead, and carried it to the carriage. While the fox was pretending to be dead. It threw all the fish on the carriage out while the hunter didn't notice, and ran away. Not until the hunter arrived home did he found out he was hoaxed by the fox.

奇趣三十三：觊觎王位雄旱獭，反客为主假殷勤

旱獭是群栖动物，每个部落里由一只德高望重、年高体强的雄旱獭担任头领。当头领渐渐年高体弱时，个别年轻气盛的雄旱獭会觊觎王位，甚至向头领挑战。不过，它即使打败了头领，众旱獭也不会拥戴它。通常在头领去世之后，大家公推一位机灵能干的雄旱獭继任。一只"野心家"旱獭见自己的部落中没有机会，只好将目光转向其他头领衰老的部落。它装作路过友邻，见到对方就点头哈腰地表示亲热，又像是向对方道歉，表示自己误入了对方的领土，然后，温顺地离开。以后，连续几天，这只雄旱獭都会光顾毗邻的领地，渐渐地就和那里的旱獭混熟了。有时它还帮助哨兵放哨，发现敌情，它第一个发出警报，并且帮助幼旱獭隐蔽；发现肥美的青草，就招呼大家去吃；见到雌旱獭，也是礼遇有加。就这样，它逐渐赢得了那个部落的信任，待到部落头领寿终正寝，它就顺理成章成了大王。

MALE MARMOT PULLING STRINGS TO BE KING

Marmots live in tribes, and every tribe has a strong and honorable male as leader. When the leader turns old, younger marmots will often aim for the "crown", or even challenge the old leader. Yet it will not win others' respect even if it wins. The new leader must be elected by others. So an aggressive male marmot had to leave its tribe and turn to weaker tribes. It pretended as a passenger, kept nodding to show his friendliness, seeming to apologize for being on the wrong land, and then left. In the coming days, it came again and again, and built a good relationship with the marmots in the new tribe. Sometimes it helped the members to defend themselves, hide their young from danger, and find food. It also treated the female marmots with respect. Days pass by and it gained the trust of the new tribe. When the leader died, it finally turned into its new "king".

点评：

从不同的角度研究动物的本能和智慧，可以发现动物有时甚至比人类更机灵。宋代著名文学家苏东坡，在

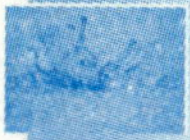

他的《黠鼠赋》中，描写过这样的一只老鼠：它被关进一个口袋里，故意吱吱乱叫，引得人们打开口袋来看，只见那只老鼠四脚朝天、双眼紧闭地躺在口袋里，大家以为它已经死去，便把它倒了出来。谁知道它一着地，便马上翻转身子，一溜烟地跑掉了，看得人们目瞪口呆。从这点便可以看出，老鼠不仅聪明，甚至还会靠玩弄诈术骗过人来挽救自己的生命。

If we give animals' instinct and wisdom an overall review, we will find that they are even smarter than people at some point. Su Shi, the great poet in Song Dynasty, once wrote "A Poem for a Clever Mouse": the mouse was captured in a bag, and it squeaked to get people's attention. People opened the bag and found it lifeless. They thought it was dead, and pulled it out. Yet it suddenly ran away after that, leaving people astonished. From that we can see, the mouse was not only smart, but also a master of tricks to save its life.

六

动物群居风景线

Stories of Animals' Group Living

风景线一：横卧泉面合欢树，蝴蝶盛会天下孤

在云南大理的卷山脚下，有一个约有10平方米的泉池，名曰蝴蝶泉。蝴蝶泉四旁用大理石栏杆围护，一杆高大的合欢树横卧泉面，每逢农历四月十五，合欢树花开满树，状如彩蝶。无数的彩蝶会群集于清泉之上，络绎不绝，如霞似绵。为此，白族人把农历四月十五定为蝴蝶会，这是蝴蝶泉一年一度的盛大节日。郭沫若《蝴蝶泉》诗中赞道："奇哉此泉天下孤。"明代徐宏祖写的《徐霞客游记》中也有记载，"其时游人如云"。

UNIQUE BUTTERFLY GATHERING ON AN ALBIZZIA ABOVE THE SPRING

Under Juan Mountain of Dali, Yunnan Province, there is a 10 square-meter fountain, named "Butterfly Fountain". It is surrounded by marble fences, with a tall acacia standing by. At April 15th of Chinese Lunar Calendar every year, butterfly-shaped flowers are blooming on the tree. Thousands of colorful butterflies will gather on the fountain, painting a marvelous picture. The Bai People has set the day as "the day of butterfly". Famous writer Guo Moruo wrote, "The unique fountain is the only one of its kind under

heaven." Xu Hongzu also wrote in his masterpiece *Travels of Xu Xiake*, that many tourists came on the day for the wonderful view.

风景线二:哥酋洛市有民俗,男女老幼皆养蛇

意大利的哥酋洛市,男女老幼都会养蛇。蛇是该城儿童的最喜爱的宠物。这个城市每年还举行一次"蛇节",节日这天,家家户户都把自己养的蛇放出来任其走街串巷,因此被人们称为"蛇城"。在这里,蛇已经成为人们社区生活的一部分。

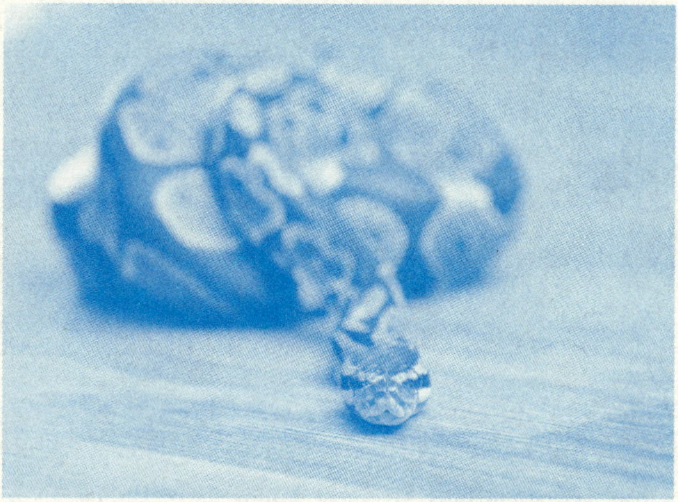

SNAKE RAISING TRADITION FOR ALL IN ITALIAN CITY

Many people, old or young, men or women, raise snakes in an Italian city. Snakes are the most favored pets for children in the city. Every year there is a Snake Day according to the tradition, on which everyone let their pet snake at large in the city. So the city is also called "Snake City". Snakes have become a part of the native life.

风景线三:峨边县内出怪事,十万青蛙大搬家

1990 年 8 月 29 日、30 日和 9 月 4 日,天上下着霏霏细雨,在四川省峨边县境内的川南森林工程局 611 伐木场附近的公路上,连续出现了三次几十万只青蛙集群搬家的怪事。这些青蛙一个背着一个,横排成行,秩序井然地跳跃行进。它们每次都是下雨时出现,顺公路行约半小时后,拐进路边的溪沟里,消失在乱石和荒草中。

COUNTLESS FROGS MOVE HOUSE NEAR EBIAN COUNTY

It was autumn of 1990; a road in Sichuan Province witnessed something strange: hundreds of thousands of frogs moved house together, three times in a row. One frog carried another on its back. They stood in rows, and jumped forward one after another. They often moved in rainy days. They travelled for half an hour, and disappeared in the gutter near the road.

风景线四：百万蟾蜍大聚会，岸上两个指挥官

1990年5月4日上午，湖南省洞口县黄桥旁约一亩水面的鱼塘里，有两只大蟾蜍登上岸像指挥官一样站在塘岸，接着，像筷子头一样大小的小癞蛤蟆“兵分两路”登岸。一路顺着6英尺宽的小巷向街上爬行，一路顺着一条二尺宽的小路向街上移动。估计一平方米约一万只小癞蛤蟆，两条共有270平方米的路面。大约有200余万只，直到下午三点多钟，这些癞蛤蟆钻地入洞后，大癞蛤蟆才随之消失。

MILLIONS OF TOADS GATHERED, LEAD BY TWO “COMMANDERS”

In the morning of May 4th, 1990, two giant toads went out of a pond in Hunan, and stood on the ground like two commanders. Then, about two million small toads moved to the land, too. They were as big as one end of a chopstick, and separated in two groups. One group moved along an alley, the other went along a small road. Not until 3 o'clock that afternoon, the small toads finished their move, did the big ones went away.

风景线五:数十万蚌聚一洞,手电照射万泉涌

在四川省某村,有一个"蚌洞",洞内生存着数十万只蚌。这个洞是水库的出口隧洞。全长 152 米,宽 1.5 米,高 1.7 米。经有关人员进洞考察,发现最大的蚌有 1.8 公斤重,最小的只有几克,估测约有 7 吨多,进洞口用手电筒照射,数万股"喷泉"就会同时喷出,在电筒光的照耀下,显得分外夺目。蚌在平时,躯体两瓣是分开的,一旦有外界影响,便立即闭合,产生喷水。

COUNTLESS CLAMS IN ONE HOLE SHOOT OUT STRINGS OF WATER WHEN FLASHED

There is a clam hole in a village of Sichuan, with thousands of clams inside. The hole belongs to a reservoir, with a length of 152 meters, a width of 1.5 meters, and a height of 1.7 meters. According to the research people who went down the hole, the largest clam in the hole weighed 1.8 kilos, while the smallest weighed only a few grams, and in total, they weighed about 7 tons. If you flash into the hole with flash light, many strands of water will come out. Usually, the two parts of a clam's shells stay open; if something happens, it will close itself and shoot out the water.

风景线六:数十万蚯蚓云集,百公斤你盘我缠

一天上午,上海地区一位农妇顾某到承包田里察看水稻,刚走近田头忽听得"沙沙"声,起先以为哪里漏水,定睛一看,不由大吃一惊,旁边一块约半亩大的旱地上,数十万条蚯蚓云集地面,你盘我缠,久久不肯散去。顾某急忙叫来乡亲,并拿出扫帚和畚箕,打扫了半个多小时,将蚯蚓收拾回家一称,重达100多公斤。

A GATHERING OF COUNTLESS EARTHWORMS

In a morning, a farmer named Gu went to her land to see the crops. She heard a strange sound, and soon found countless earthworms tangling with each other in the field nearby. She was astonished by the scene, and called upon others to clean them away. The earthworms they got at that day weighted more than 100 kilos.

风景线七：蚊子聚会秧田边，绕柱旋转像烟囱

1985 年初夏，在河南省一处秧田边，发生过一次蚊子大聚会。这是由不计其数的蚊子组成的奇观。它形成了直径约 2 尺，高约 30 丈的大柱体，这些蚊子以顺时针方向边叫边旋转。“柱子”中间形成一个空洞，就像是用蚊子堆砌的大烟囱一样。

MOSQUITO PARTY NEAR A FIELD FORMING A CYLINDER

On early summer of 1985, a grand gathering of mosquitos took place near a field in Henan Province. It was a wonder by countless mosquitos. There was a cylinder with a diameter of about 70 centimeters, and a height of around 100 meters formed by flying mosquitos. They flew clockwise, buzzing. The cylinder had a cavity in the middle, like a chimney made of the insect.

风景线八：南美食肉蚁大军，所向披靡集团

南美洲食肉蚁褐色的身体，虽然只有半个拇指大，但嘴巴可以在瞬间咬穿几层衣服。1883 年的一天，在巴西亚马逊河畔曾出现一支庞大的食肉蚁大军。这群食肉大军排列成长 10 公里，宽 5 公里的方阵，所向披靡，并肩在河面上用力向对岸游去。蚁群所经过的地方，四处一片寂静，只有它们身体移动的沙沙声。一只体重 60 公斤的母豹子，在它们经过时，不到 4 分钟就只剩下一堆白骨。

SOUTH AMERICAN CANNIBAL ANTS RUN WILD AS A GROUP

The brown body of South American cannibal ant has the size of only half of our thumb, but its mouth has the power to bite through several layers of clothes. In 1883, a large cannibal ant army appeared near Amazon River in Brazil. They were in a rectangle with a length of 10 kilometers and a width of 5. They swam across the river shoulder against shoulder, leaving nothing on their path but the rustling sound. They passed through a 60-kilo female leopard, and it turned to bones after only 4 minutes.

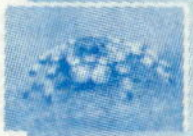

风景线九：鼓虾能分敌和友，长者保卫任务重

美国佛吉尼亚州威廉和玛丽学院海洋科学院的生态学家达菲在加勒比海长有海绵的礁石群中发现，每个鼓虾群相对独立地生活在海绵体中。同时，鼓虾能区分“敌友”，每个群落中岁数较大的虾担负着保卫“虾王”和幼虾的责任。当他把其他群落的鼓虾或其他种类的虾放进某个鼓虾群落中时，鼓虾们总是挥舞着钳子，奋勇抵御外来敌人。有时几只鼓虾还会联合起来，用钳子钳住敌人并将它们拖出虾群生活的海绵体。

SHRIMPS DEFEND FRIENDS AND DEFEAT FOES

Ecologist Duffy of William and Mary Institute of Oceanology in Virginia, US, found in the reefs in Caribbean, that in the sponge of the reefs, there lived many independent tribes of a kind of shrimp. They can tell enemies from friends. The oldest shrimp in every tribe guards its “king” and young members. When the scientist put a shrimp into another tribe, the members of the tribe would use their pliers to pull it out from the sponge they lived in.

风景线十：碧水蓝天青海湖，安居乐业鸟世界

青海湖碧波蓝天，湖水中有丰富的鱼虾和水草。湖周围的大草原一望无际，又没有野兽侵扰，是各种飞鸟安居乐业的天堂。1959 年 9 月，我国动物学家在青海湖发现了一个叫做海西皮的小岛，面积约四百多亩。岛上有各种各样的鸟，铺天盖地。每年的夏季，有一百多种鸟来这里“生儿育女”。几千年来，在这座幽静的湖畔成了一座“鸟的城市”。我国已把这座鸟岛列为“鸟岛水禽保护区”。

QINGHAI LAKE, A HEAVEN FOR BIRDS

Qinhai Lake has rich resources of water living creatures. The vast grassland near it without prayers is a heaven for all kinds of birds. In Sept. 1959, an island named Haixipi was found by some Chinese zoologists. The 400-*mu* island has many kinds of birds on it. Every summer, more than 100 birds flies to the island to brood. After thousands of years, a city of birds was built near the quiet lake. China has listed the island "Protection Zone of Waterfowl".

风景线十一:印度洋上有奇岛,满地皆是海燕蛋

在印度洋的塞舌尔群岛中,有一个面积四十多公顷的小岛,每年七月,成群结队的海燕大批飞到岛上做窝、配偶、生蛋、孵化。繁殖期一过,海燕们又携儿带眷,展翅高飞了。

1930 年,有 170 万对海燕"情侣"在岛上下蛋,结果岛上的海燕蛋俯拾皆是,由此"蛋岛"而得名。从那以后,岛上的居民,有的就以拾蛋为生。蛋商加工后,销往国外,一年可出口海燕蛋 420 万只左右,在国际市场享有盛名。

STRANGE INDONESIAN ISLANDS FULL OF PETREL EGGS

Among the Islands of Seychelles on Indian Ocean, a small island of more than 40 hectares has flocks of petrels to brood on it every July. After the breeding period, they fly away together with their families.

The island is called "Egg Island" for in 1990, eggs laid by more than 1.7 million couples of petrels almost flooded the island. From then on, the islanders live on collecting eggs. It enjoyed international reputation for its egg exportation of 4.2 million a year.

点评：

动物同人类一样具有一定的“社会性”。昆虫学家发现，对于群居的动物来说，孤独会使它们忧伤；有些昆虫如果没有同类的陪伴还会死亡。比如，蚂蚁和蜜蜂的伙伴不能少于25个，如果少于25个，这些习惯于正常群居的动物就会感到非常忧伤。美国科学家自1984年至1999年，对生活在肯尼亚安波塞里国家公园里的108只雌狒狒，进行了长达15年的悉心观察发现，喜欢聚堆的雌狒狒，每天要花十分之一的时间来聚会碰面。本来，狒狒们可以利用更多的时间和体力来采集食物、侦察情况、喂养子女或培养子女的生存能力等等。但它们并没有这样做。或许动物之间已经越来越需要社会性的接触，因为它们最清楚适者生存的法则，或许它们已越来越清醒地意识到，为了使自己家族更好地繁衍下去，加强群体间的交流，是防止血缘断绝最好的手段。他们还发现那些喜欢聚堆的雌狒狒的生育死亡率低得多，

Just as human, animals are social, too. Entomologists found out that for social animals, loneliness can cause pain, or even death. Like ants and bees can only survive with friends of more than 25. A 15-year research on 108 female gorillas in Amboseli National Park of Kenya by American scientists showed that social gorillas spend 1/10 of time every day to meet with each other. They could have used the time on foraging, brooding or investigation, but they chose to keep social, for their natural needs perhaps. They might have known the rule "survival of the fittest", and to gain communication between groups can help precede their kind. A research also found that social female gorillas have lower labor mortality rate.

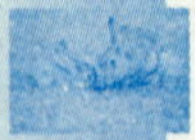

七

动物家庭风景线

Family Stories of Animals

风景线——:狮子家宴等级严,不听指挥就撵走

一群狮子在举行家宴时,有一只幼狮不听指挥,想自己拖走一块肉独享,雄狮顿时翻脸,立马下一道“逐客令”把它撵走了。原来狮子的家族等级非常严格,一族之主的雄狮,每次撕碎猎物后,要先独自享受一番,然后再让雌狮和幼狮去吃。如有哪个吃得不老实的,雄狮就会一阵张牙舞爪,严加“训斥”。

CLASS DIFFERENCES ON LION FAMILY BANQUETS

Once, a family of lions was holding a banquet. A young lion tried to get a piece of meat for itself. A male lion drove it away at once. Lion families have strict class differences. The male leader of the family enjoys the right of dining first when it gets food, and then gives it to the female and young. If anyone in the family tries to get more than it deserved, the male lion will "scold" it harshly.

风景线二：下蛋母鸡失踪影，拖儿带女把家还

1992 年 11 月 2 日，上海地区一位农户乔某家里一只下蛋的母鸡突然失踪。主人对此也没在意，估计是被黄鼠狼叼走了。然而，65 天后的一个上午，这只老母鸡竟然回到家里，并且带回了一窝自己孵化的 11 只幼鸡。原来，这只母鸡为了避免下的蛋被主人吃掉，有意离家出走，在不远的田埂里做窝孵蛋，有了后代以后，才返回主人家。

LOST HEN RETURNED WITH ITS CHILDREN

On Nov. 2ed, 1992, a brooding hen disappeared from a farmer Qiao's house. The owner didn't pay much attention to it, and he thought it was stolen by some weasel. While after 65 days, the hen returned, with 11 children it brooded. It was afraid that its eggs would have been eaten by the owner, so it went away from home, brooded in the near field, and returned when its

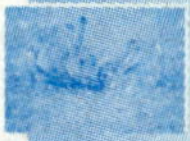

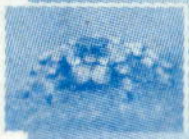

children were hatched.

风景线三：坦桑尼亚大狒狒，自主营建“托儿所”

在非洲坦桑尼亚的大森林里，群居着一种狒狒。当狒狒七八个月断奶后，如果母亲要出去觅食等，便把“孩子”送到“托儿所”，也就是交给一位年长的雌狒狒看管。“托儿所”里的“阿姨”尽职尽责，从不准小狒狒们乱跑，还教它们丢石块、爬树、游泳等活动。

GORILLA IN TANZANIA HAS A NURSERY

In the forest of Tanzania, Africa, gorillas send their children to a“nursery” when they go out hunting, which is to have a senior female gorilla take care of them. The child-care workers are dutiful to their jobs. They keep the little gorillas in line, and teach them to throw stones, climb trees and swim.

风景线四：实行岗位责任制，集体管理幼企鹅

在企鹅的家庭里，为了不让自己未出壳的小宝宝落到雪地上被冻，实行了岗位责任制，也就是雌雄企鹅轮流用脚抱蛋。

有趣的是幼企鹅出生后 30～60 天左右的时间内，为

了幼企鹅得到保护和看管,同时又不影响它们长期劳累的父母能放心地去海中觅食,老企鹅们会组成的一个团队,一起照顾刚孵化的小企鹅。

YOUNG PENGUINS RAISED BY GROUP PERFORMING POST RESPONSIBILITY

Penguin parents adopt post responsibility system to keep their babies from the cold ice, which is to hold the eggs in turn by their feet.

In 30～60 days after the penguin babies are born, their parents have to go away to find food. So the senior penguins form a group to take the new-born babies together.

风景线五：同室理应阖家亲，燕窝演绎母子情

辽宁省营口市一座办公楼的楼檐下曾有一个燕窝，里面有五只毛茸茸的小燕。一天，五只小燕飞出燕窝“放风”，回窝时，四只淘气的小燕在窝里左右摇晃身子不让第五只燕子归巢，这只小燕子见此情景，愤然离家出走。不一会儿，母燕回窝见少了一只小燕，先是叽叽喳喳“训”了四只小燕一通，此时，窝里的四只小燕默不作声。然后，母燕飞了出去，召集了十几只燕子帮助寻找小燕。燕群在二十多米的半径内低空飞行寻找目标。十五分钟左右，伴着欢快的燕叫声，母燕带着小燕子飞了回来。母子俩先是落在燕窝附近的砖墙上，母燕用嘴不停地啄着小燕的头部，表示安抚。几只受母燕“训”的小燕则规规矩矩，主动向一侧靠拢，给这“走失”的小燕腾出了一块落脚的地方。

MOTHER'S LOVE IN SWALLOW NEST

Under the roof of an office building in Yinkou City, Liaoning Province, there was a swallow nest, with five little swallows living inside. One day when they returned to the nest after playing, four of them wobbled in the nest to keep the fifth out. The fifth was angry with its brothers and sisters, so it left home. When their mother returned, and found one of its children missing, it "scolded" the four in the nest, and called upon dozens of others to find its child. They flew low in a 20-meter diameter, and found the target in 15 minutes. The mother touched the young on its head to comfort it. Its brothers and sisters quietly moved away to let it in the nest.

风景线六:黄鼠共贮御冬粮,恩爱夫妻似人类

北方有一种小黄鼠,实行严格的一夫一妻制,洞穴中的小土窑,好似床塌一般,就是它们的婚床。平日里,它们共同准备御冬的食物,分别用小土窑贮存起来。每当天气晴朗时,它们坐在洞口,看见人来,则拱动前脚,像"作揖"一样,随时准备逃回洞穴中,因此,人们又称它为"礼鼠"。

YELLOW MICE STORE FOOD TOGETHER FOR WINTER LIKE HUMAN

A yellow mouse in the north has strict monogamy. They live in caves, and collect mud to make their wedding bed. They find food for winter in usual days, and store it with mud. In sunny days they fold their front feet together and wave them, like bowing, to prepare for running back to the cave. People also call them "courtesy mouse".

风景线七：濑鱼家庭真有趣，妻子摇身变丈夫

澳大利亚堤礁的海水里，有一种色彩艳丽的濑鱼。雄濑鱼非常好斗，沿袭着"一夫多妻"的制度。平常，雄濑鱼雄赳赳地捍卫着自己的"领土"，守卫着自己 7～9 个"妻妾"。它沿着自己的领土巡视的时候，便让她们排成一队，尾随在后。而她们中通常有一条会"指手画脚"，支配"别人"。但一旦这条雄濑鱼死了，数小时后，那一条喜欢指挥别人的雌濑鱼便开始接替丈夫的地位，并且在一个月之内，就会在生理上也完全变成了雄濑鱼。

WIFE TURNS INTO HUSBAND IN WRASSE FAMILY

In the barrier reef of Australian sea, lives a kind of colorful wrasse. The male wrasses are aggressive, and they adopt polygamy. Usually, a male wrasse patrols its land and protects its 7～9 "wives". When it patrols it keeps the females in a line to follow behind. Some of the females like to boss around others, and when the male dies the most dominant female will take its place, and turn into a male in one month.

点评:

家庭是人类社会的细胞。动物的家庭同人类的家庭有很多相似之处。在动物世界,家庭作为维系血缘关系的纽带,既体现了夫妻恩爱、母子情深、共同合作;也展示了严格的家庭管理和“等级制度”。

Families are cells of human society. Animal world is similar to that of human. Family is also the bond of blood. It shows love between parents and children, husband and wife, strict family management and social levels.

八

动物教育方法记趣

Education Stories of Animals

记趣一：一鼠毙命新鼠药，全城老鼠不上当

法国有位科学家曾把一种剧毒的新鼠药放入巴黎的一个下水道中，有一只老鼠只吃了一口，当即毙命。旁边的几只老鼠目睹同伙被毒死，便赶快离开了。几天之后，消息就在全城的老鼠中传开了。之后，无论把新鼠药放在哪一个排水沟中，也再没有一只老鼠接触它。科学家因此认为，老鼠是能够通过互相学习和沟通来增长知识，可以把对新事物的好恶与同伴进行交流。

MICE SHARE INFORMATION ABOUT NEW POISON

A French scientist once put a new kind of mouse poison in a sewer of Paris, and a mouse died for that. A few other mice witnessed that and ran away quickly. In a few days the news about the new poison spread among mice around the city. From then on, no matter the researchers put the poison in which sewer, no mouse touched it again. The researchers thought that mice could gain knowledge through communication and study, to exchange opinions on new things.

记趣二：适者生存小企鹅，父母边跑边喂食

企鹅在给刚刚学会走路的小企鹅喂食的时候，总是在跑步中完成的。企鹅的父母明白在食物匮乏的南极大陆，那些体弱的、跑不快的小企鹅，根本得不到充分的食物，迟早都会饿死，所以它们选择了一边跑一边喂食的方法，训练小企鹅奔跑的能力。

PENGUINS FEED BABIES RUNNING SHOWING "SURVIVAL OF THE FITTEST"

When little penguins just learn to walk, their parents feed them when they are running together. They know that in the harsh environment, the penguins that are too weak to run fast cannot get enough food and die very soon. So they choose to feed them while running, to train their children to be a fast runner.

记趣三：奔驰草原母猎豹，实战现场育后代

在非洲寥廓的大草原上，猎豹捕捉到受伤的羚羊或斑马后，不是马上咬死，而是有意地放它逃走。接着敦促尾随过来的小猎豹前去追赶猎物。小猎豹稍有懈怠，母豹便会毫不留情地加以扑打、驱赶，直到它们明白母亲的用意，抖擞精神，奋力追赶受伤的猎物方才罢休。

LEOPARDS TEACH CHILDREN HUNTING IN BATTLE

On the vast African prairie, when a leopard catches a wounded antelope or zebra, it will not kill the prey, but let them run first, and ask the little leopards to kill them. If the children don't work hard enough, the parents will harshly punish them until they run after the preys with full energy.

记趣四：教育幼狐获食物，循序渐进讲方法

狐狸对自己孩子的教育更有系统性。第一步它们将咬死的田鼠放在幼子身上，让它们各自去咬、去打。第二步是鼓励孩子相互争夺食物。第三步要求孩子们与负伤的田鼠格斗。最后是实战，带它们到树林、田野中去捕捉

田鼠。正是出于对幼狐的关爱，成狐才有这份耐心，尽心尽力地教育小狐狸学会独立获取食物之道。

GRADUAL LESSONS FOR BABY FOXES ON PREYING

Foxes have a systematical education for its children on preying. Firstly they give the dead voles to the young for biting. Secondly they let the children fight with each other for food. Then the children are trained to fight wounded voles. At last the little foxes are taken to the field and catch the voles by themselves. The patience of the adult foxes is due to their love and care to the young ones.

点评：

教育是培养新生一代准备从事社会生活的整个过程。动物同人类一样，在漫长的动物进化过程中，为了种族的延续和发展，非常重视经验的交流和学习。同时，它们还懂得从各自不同的生理特征和生活环境出发，总结出一套符合本物种特点的教育方法，以培养它们的后代更好适应自然、学会生存。

Education aims at helping the young prepare for their social lives. Just like human, animals pay attention to communication and learning for the development and continuation of its kind, in the long process of evolvement. They can also summarize from their own characters and living environment to get the best teaching policy for their children, to make them better at accommodation and survival.

九

动物计划生育记趣

Stories of Animal Birth Control

记趣一：非洲羚羊有本领，推迟分娩两月半

非洲羚羊也具有控制生育本领。雌羚羊若“阴差阳错”地受孕怀胎过早，它们能推迟分娩时 77 天，把快分娩的胎儿继续留在腹内，等到春暖花开、万物生长的季节到来时再产下幼仔。

AFRICAN ANTELOPES CAN DELAY LABOR FOR 77 DAYS

African Antelopes have the ability of birth control. If they have an unplanned baby, they can delay the birth of the child by 77 days, so it can be born on warm spring days.

记趣二：啮齿动物婚配后，优生优育选时光

貂鼠、花斑臭鼬等啮齿类动物夏秋天婚配后，健康的受精卵可暂停发育，呈囊胚状态浮动在子宫里面，等到冬去春来食物十分丰富，生理上又做好了怀孕生产准备时，母兽这才使受精卵附着在子宫壁上发育成胚胎。

RODENTS CHOOSE LABOR TIME WISELY AFTER MATING

Female rodents like martens and skunks can stop the development of their healthy germ cells after their mating in summer or autumn. It will flow in their uterus in the state of blastosphere. When spring comes, they will have abundant food, and their bodies are more prepared for the labor. That is the time for females to let the germ cell flow to the wall of their uterus to develop into a fetus.

记趣三：英国老鼠选美赛，优生繁殖比成果

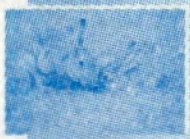

英国二十年前就成立了“全国老鼠协会”，其宗旨是要在全国推行“老鼠优生繁殖”，约有会员 200 余人。每年大约要有 40 次“老鼠选美大赛”，其赛事主要在伦敦和

约克郡举行。英国的养鼠爱好者醉心的游戏就是替老鼠配种，然后在选美大赛中相互拿各自的“成果”作比较，看谁配出的品种最优良最美丽。

BEAUTY PAGEANT OF MICE IN THE GREAT BRITAIN

20 years ago the Great Britain settled “the national community of mice” with about 200 members, to improve mouse reproduction nationally. Every year they hold more than 40 “Beauty Pageant of Mice”, mainly in London and Yorkshire. Mice breeding has become an interesting game for British mouse lovers, they compare the breeds with each other to choose a winner.

记趣四：内蒙草原野盘羊，本能忌讳近亲配

在内蒙古北部的莽莽草原上，生长着一种野盘羊，是国家一级保护动物，身躯健壮，生性凶猛。这种野盘羊本能地忌讳“近亲交配”，在找不到同类异性的情况下，雄性野盘羊就掺入家羊群当“女婿”。

INNER MONGOLIA ARGALI KNOWS TO AVOID INTERMARRIGE

On the prairie of Inner Mongolia lives an argali. It is one of the 1st grade national protection animals, with strong body and fierce nature. They are born with an instinct to avoid “intermarriage”. If they cannot find a mate in its own kind, male argali will “marry” one of the domestic sheep.

记趣五：京燕择木而栖之，优生优育讲方法

法国和瑞典的学者通过对瑞典哥特兰岛上的一种京燕进行跟踪研究发现，新婚的京燕夫妇在选择筑巢孵蛋的地点时，往往会参照其他鸟类的经验。如果某片树林中其他鸟类的雏鸟数量多且健壮，京燕夫妻也会在这里安家。科学家由此得出结论：“生殖成功”是鸟类选择栖

息地的重要标准。为了验证这猜想，科学家又进行了一次试验。他们将出生只有七天的小鸟搬到别的鸟巢中，人为地造成某片树林适合鸟类生儿育女的假象，结果真有越来越多的京燕来这里筑巢产蛋。

SWALLOW CHOOSES WHERE IT BROODS AND KNOWS EUGENICS

A research by French and Swedish experts about a swallow on Gotland, Sweden, shows that the newly-wed swallows will learn from the experience of other birds when they build their nests. If they see many healthy young birds in a forest, they will stay here, too. The researchers think that the choice of brooding place by birds is due to reproduction. Two other experiments were carried out: the experts put some newly hatched birds in a forest to make it look like a fine place to breed, to see whether the swallows choose the place to build the nest. Not surprisingly, they actually did.

记趣六：整批沉海怪旅鼠，优胜劣汰讲优生

挪威的旅鼠每隔三到四年，便会有一种奇怪的行为。它们由山上俯冲下来，头向着海，跳进水中，然后整批沉没。它们为什么要集体自杀，至今仍是自然之谜。一位

美国科学家用营养恢复学说来解释这种自杀：当鼠类数量达到高峰时，植被因遭到过度啃食而被破坏，食物不足、隐蔽条件恶化，于是它们只好留下少数优秀的旅鼠以繁衍后代，其他都要自尽。等到植被恢复时，它们的数量又会节节攀升。

STRANGE LEMMINGS SUICIDE FOR EUGENICS

Lemmings in Norway conduct a strange behavior every three to four years: they rush down the mountain to the sea, and then drown. The reason for the suicide is still a misery. An American scientist tried to explain it by nutrient recovery hypothesis, that when the number of lemmings reaches the peak, the plants will be destroyed, and there will be no place to hide. The only way is to leave a small number of lemmings with better genes, and let the rest kill themselves. When more plants grow back, their number increases again.

点评：

人们普遍认为，动物主要靠本能繁衍后代。但是，随着人类认识能力的提高，科学家们发现，动物为了顺应“适者生存”的自然法则，目前世界上有100多种哺乳动物能巧妙地实行“计划生育”。非洲大象就能根据当地食物供求的情况决定多生还是少生。譬如，在尼罗河一侧，

由于树木茂盛，食物丰富，母象每隔四年就可以生一胎；而在尼罗河的另一侧，由于环境恶劣，食物来源困难，母象就相隔九年才生一胎。当然，它们为了达到优生优育，一些动物还会采用极端的行为。由此可见，“计划生育”并非人类的专利。

It is common to think that animals reproduce by instinct. While as we know more about animals, we find that more than 100 mammals adopt family planning methods according to the “survival of the fittest” law. African elephants decide when to have children by food production: one side of the Nile River has rich forest and plenty of food, so the elephants have one child about every four years; while on the other side with less food, they labor as long as every nine years. Some animals even take extreme actions to improve their reproduction quality. Therefore, not only people take family planning actions.

十

动物服务人类的故事

Stories about Animals Helping People

故事一：军中神犬建战功，退役改行当医生

2000 年 3 月，牧羊犬"切恩"在接受专业训练不满 3 年的情况下，凭借敏锐的嗅觉协助"阿尔法"队员一举捣毁了车臣恐怖分子的地下巢穴。从那以后，"切恩"便多次查处车匪暗藏的武器弹药。为此，"切恩"与其恩师屡次受到上级嘉奖。

2005 年春，"切恩"年满 8 岁，到了军犬的"退休年龄"。按照规定，退休后，它每月可以领取 1200 卢布。虽然退休，"切恩"也没闲着，它又在一家康复中心做起了"狗医生"。这位"狗医生"对前来就诊的孩子非常体贴。它时而温顺的伏在病人的怀里，时而舔舔病人的手和脸，使那些久坐轮椅、目光呆滞的孩子的脸上露出难得的笑容。

ARMY DOG WITH MEDALS BECAME DOCTOR AFTER SERVICE

On March 2000, a shepherd dog "Cheyne", with less than 3 years' training, helped "Alpha" members destroyed an underground Chechnya terrorist base with its excellent smell. After that, it often helped find hidden guns and explosive weapons. Cheyne and its trainer were awarded for many times for that.

When Cheyene was eight, in spring 2005, it retired. It could get 1200 roubles every month according to the regulations. It became a "dog doctor" in a rehabilitation center. It cared much about the young patients. It sometimes stayed in their arms, sometimes licked their faces and hands. The dull-eyed children in armchairs came into smile after seeing it.

故事二：鸵鸟牧羊开普敦，听从命令能力强

非洲开普敦牧场用鸵鸟来牧羊。非洲鸵鸟高约 2.75 米，长约 2 米，重量 90 公斤，是世界上最大的鸟。它头颈很长，翅膀却很短，不会飞翔，但奔跑起来连快马也赶不上。它虽不如狗灵敏，但经驯服，便很听使唤，"责任心"强，还有股蛮劲。窃贼跑来偷羊，只要鸵鸟发现了，就马

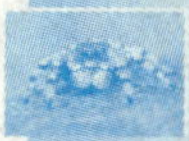

上迈开长腿飞奔过去，将窃贼赶走。有时鸵鸟还会过于卖力，看到汽车驶过时，也会当作窃贼，穷追不舍。

RESPONSIBLE OSTRICH SHEPHERDS IN CAPE TOWN

Ostriches are used for shepherd in Cape Town, Africa. They are the largest birds in the world, about 2.75 meters in height and 2 meters in length, and weigh about 90 kilograms. They have long necks and short wings, cannot play but run very fast. They are not as agile as dogs, but are obedient, responsible and strong. When they find thieves try to steal sheep, they will drive them away at once. Sometimes they even take cars as thieves, and run after them, too.

故事三:狒狒牧羊真卖力,认真点数又喂奶

非洲某牧羊场,人们驯养狒狒来牧羊。狒狒每天赶着羊群去吃草,太阳落山时,认真点数后,又赶着羊群回家。发现少了羊,就发出叫声,唤迷途的羔羊回来。母羊回栏后,羔羊直叫唤,狒狒就主动抱起小羊,送过去吃奶。

DILIGENT GORILLAS SHEPHERDS LEAVING NONE BEHIND

Gorillas are also used for shepherd in Africa. They drive the sheep to grassland In the morning, and drive them home at sundown. They count the sheep carefully, and howl to call the ones that run too far back. Little sheep often cry after returning, and the gorillas carry them to their mothers for breast-feed.

故事四:青蛙举重在美国,赢得满场喝彩声

美国加利福尼亚州曾举行过一次别开生面的青蛙举重表演。只见一只经驯化后的青蛙仰面而躺,用两爪举起一副特制的杠铃。样子十分轻松自如,赢得了满场喝彩。

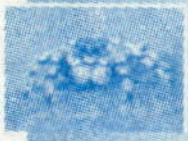

CHEERS FOR FROG WEIGHT-LIFTING IN CALIFORNIA

A frog weight-lifting show was held in California, US. A trained frog lay on the floor and lifted a special barbell with ease. All the audience applauded and cheered.

故事五:美国 10 岁杂种狗,水面滑行技术高

在美国迈阿密市有一条名叫“斯科奇”的杂种狗非常机灵。在当地消防队员,业余滑水爱好者德鲁·凯思的精心训练下,这条 10 岁的狗只用几个星期的时间就掌握了一般人难以掌握的滑水技术。滑水时“斯科奇”将滑板的绳子衔在嘴里,就能在水面上滑行。

A HYBRID DOG'S FANTASTIC WATER-SAILING SKILLS

A 10-year-old hybrid dog in Miami, US, was very smart. After the training of local firefighter Drew Keith, the dog mastered the water-sailing skills that untrained people cannot do. It sailed with its teeth biting into the rope.

故事六:长跑之邦肯尼亚,陪跑队员是鸵鸟

在有"长跑之邦"美称的非洲国度肯尼亚,国家田径队训练时利用鸵鸟来陪跑。在训练中运动员要力求抓住鸵鸟的尾巴,受过专门训练的陪跑鸵鸟,好像懂事似的,总是领先运动员 2 米,运动员加速,它加速。经过一段时间的鸵鸟陪跑训练后,运动员的中长跑成绩都会大大提高。

OSTRICHES RUN WITH TRAINING ATHLETES IN KENYA

In Kenya, "the nation of long-distance running", national athletes run with ostriches in training. The athletes grab their tails, and they keep leading for about 2 meters. When the athletes run faster, they speed up, too. Those who run with ostriches for some time all get better achievements in races.

故事七：猩猩组成足球队，世界各地去表演

在奥地利，有一位名叫古伯勒的驯兽师，驯养了四只黑猩猩踢足球。他经常带着这四只训练有素的黑猩猩到各国旅行，并进行专场表演。每次表演，四只黑猩猩都攻防有法，惟妙惟肖，赢得观众满堂喝彩。

GORILLA FOOTBALL TEAM'S WORLD PERFORM

In Austria, an animal trainer named Waley Gubler trained four gorillas to play football. He often takes them to travel around the world and perform. The gorillas play the ball with strategy in every "match". All the audience cheered for them every time.

故事八：美国猴子足球队，场上奔走追逐忙

美国加利福尼亚洲红本野生动物园为了吸引游客，组织了一支猴子足球队。这些猴子身穿球衣球裤，脚穿鞋袜，在场上奔走追逐，互不相让。观众在观看猴子踢足球时，允许向场内掷香蕉、苹果和花生等食品，作为对猴子的奖励。

AMERICAN MONKEY FOOTBALL TEAM BUSY ON FIELD

An animal park organized a monkey football team to attract more visitors. The monkeys wear full football outfit and scramble against each other. The audience is allowed to throw peanuts, apples or bananas into the pit, to reward the monkeys.

故事九：体育表演在美国，拳击对手是袋鼠

美国新墨西哥州举行一年一度的体育表演。在拳击台上，一只受过拳击训练的袋鼠“洛奇”正与一名拳手对垒。只见袋鼠用戴着特制手套的右前肢向前一击，正中拳手的前额，令拳手难以招架。

BOXING SHOW WITH KANGAROO IN THE US

An annual sports show in New Mexican, US had a special boxing show when a kangaroo fought with a boxer. The kangaroo wore a special glove, and hit the forehead of the boxer. That was a hard blow to take!

故事十：澳大利亚螃蟹赛，不准喝彩不准喊

在澳大利亚的一座岛上，每年举办一次螃蟹比赛。比赛开始前，主人先把螃蟹扣在一个水桶下面，当黄灯亮起，主人就把水桶掀开，螃蟹就争先恐后地沿着跑道向前奔跑。观众们看螃蟹赛跑，不能鼓掌，不准喝彩，只能屏住呼吸，暗暗为螃蟹加油。因为如果人们大叫大喊，就会吓得螃蟹停止不前，或跑出规定的跑道。如果出现这种情况，比赛就得重新开始。

A QUIET RACE OF CRABS IN AUSTRALIA

On an island of Australia, every year there is a crab racing contest. The host keeps the crabs under a bucket, and when a yellow light is on, he lets the crabs go. They run fast ahead, while the audience was not allowed to cheer or applaud, for the noise may scare the crabs, and the race had to start again.

故事十一：泰国举办斗猪赛，最后取胜获奖金

在泰国叻丕府每年的泼水节期间，都要举办斗猪比赛。首先是淘汰赛，接着从中选出五对优利者进行决赛。猪在拼斗时，十分勇猛，场面紧张而热烈。每场观众都有数千人。比赛优胜者的主人可获得一笔可观的奖金。

PIG FIGHTING IN THAILAND WITH BIG AWARD

Ratchaburi Province of Thailand has a pig fighting contest every year during the Water-spilling Festival. First the knockout match, and then the final match among the five winners. Pigs are fierce when fighting, and the match is tense. Thousands of people come to see the match, and the winner's owner can get a large amount of award.

故事十二：功绩卓著—信鸽，战后英国授勋章

二战中，盟军诺曼底登陆成功的消息首先是由英国皇家的一只信鸽传递给后方的。2004 年，英国人给它以至高荣誉。这只信鸽名叫"古斯塔夫"，在空军中的代号是 NPS4231066。在它诞生 60 周年纪念日到来之际，帝国战争博物馆举行了特殊仪式，为其授勋。

当年，古斯塔夫从法国诺曼底出发，在乌云密布的恶劣天气条件下，顶着时速 48 公里的大风，在 5 小时 15 分钟的时间内飞行 150 海里，抵达南部海岸的索尼岛。它携带的纸条写着："我们距海岸只有 20 海里，第一批队伍在 7 点 50 分发动了进攻。信号尚未显示海滩上有敌人火力。我们已排好阵势等待指令。从 5 点 45 分开始出现闪电和台风，尚未发现敌方飞机。"古斯塔夫因此而获得迪根勋章。

PIGEON AWARDED METAL IN BRITAIN AFTER WAR

In the World War Two, the news of the Normandy Landing was sent to the rear by a pigeon of the British Royals. In 2004 it was given the highest honor. Its name was "Gustavo", its code was NPS4231066. At the 60th anniversary of its birth, the Imperial War Museum hold a special ceremony to honor it.

At that time, Gustavo started at Normandy, flew 150 sea miles for 5 hours and 15 minutes, against the wind of 48km/h, and reached the Sony Island in the southern coast. The note it carried wrote, "We are only 20 sea meters from coast, and the first attack will start at 0750. Signals have not shown enemy forces on coast. We are fully prepared for commands. Lightening and storm have appeared since 0545, with no signs of enemy flights." Gustavo was awarded the Deakins Medal for this.

故事十三：公鸡掌柜叫阿滑，文具店里好助手

泰国曼谷一家书报文具店的店主，养了一只叫"阿滑"的大公鸡，它每天凌晨5点即放声啼鸣，催促主人起床。店主给"阿滑"吃过早餐后，把它放书报摊上，它就会精神抖擞地看守书报摊。于是店主便放心地去照管别的柜台或做其他事。若顾客购买书报，"阿滑"便会发出"咕咕"的叫声，店主闻声即来将书报拿给顾客。若有人乱拿乱动书报，"阿滑"就伸出利爪，把他抓得皮破血流。

ROOSTER A HUA HELPED IN STATIONARY STORE

The owner of a stationary store kept a rooster named A Hua, which crowed every morning at 5. The owner prepared the breakfast of the rooster, put it on the newspaper stand and went away for other businesses. It guarded the stand with a high spirit. If customers want newspaper or books, it clucks so that the owner would come out to cater the customers. If anyone tried to steal something away, A Hua would use its claws to teach him a lesson.

故事十四：汝拉山下铁道口，猩猩充当扳道工

在法国东部汝拉山 92 英里处铁道口的小屋里住着一位老扳道工，有一只大猩猩不知何时起经常光顾老人的小破屋。每次，老人都给它食物，结果猩猩干脆住下不走了，和老人成了朋友。在老人的训练下，大猩猩不仅会提水、扫地、烧火，而且还学会了扳道岔和向往来的火车举信号旗。

几年后的一天，老人不幸被暴风雪卷进山谷身亡，但这里像什么事也没发生一样，来往列车照常安全通过，司机们仍旧可以看见那个其貌不扬却十分可爱的家伙立在小屋前，在寒风里高举着老旧的信号旗。铁路部门不得不允许它继续工作，并让新来的扳道工住在附近，协助猩猩工作并负责为它提供食物。

SWITCH-GORILLA OF JURA MOUNTAIN RAILWAY CROSSING

A senior switchman lived in a house 92 kilometers from Jura Mountain, east of France. A gorilla came to his house very often since a long time ago, and finally stayed in the cabin. The old man trained it to fetch water, sweep floor and make fire, as well as switch the railway and wave signal flags.

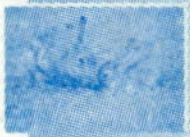

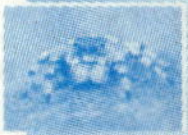

A few years later, the old man died in a snow storm, while trains passed the place as usual. The drivers a cute little guy standing in front of the cabin, waving an old signal flag in the cold winds. The railway department had to let it go on to work, and asked the new switchman to live near, helping the work and supplying it with food.

故事十五：商店老板出奇招，两只毒蜘守店门

伦敦一家百货商店的老板哈斯维尔，每晚用两只毒蜘蛛替他守店。说来也怪，这种毒蜘蛛把门，盗贼纷纷逃遁，几年来该店未曾丢失过任何东西。

无独有偶，美国某家珠宝店为了防贼，特地在橱窗内挂上警告牌，称店里饲养着专门守护珠宝的蜘蛛，如果贼人胆敢偷盗，后果自负。

POISONOUS SPIDER STORE GUARDS

Haswell was the owner of a shop in London. He hired two poisonous spiders to guard the store. It was surprising that the thieves never came since then.

An American jewelry store also had a signal board in its shopping-window, stating that the store had guard spiders inside, and they could do anything to the thieves if they dare break in.

故事十六:太平洋岛小吠蛙,看守门户如恶狗

在太平洋一座群岛上,有一种很小的青蓝色的青蛙。别看它小,却能发出很响亮的叫声,丝毫不亚于恶狗的狂吠声,正是由于这一特点,吠蛙被宠物商挖掘,提供给人们作看守门户之用。当它守护主人门户时,一旦有陌生人入户,就会发出清脆的叫声,引起主人的注意。

BARKING FROG GUARDS ON A PACIFIC ISLAND

On the islands on Pacific Ocean, there is a small frog with green and blue skin. They are tiny but can bark in a loud voice. They were found by the petshop owners, and used for guarding. When someone enters the house they are guarding, it barks so that the owner will notice.

故事十七：非洲大象消防队，行动迅速奔火场

在非洲突尼斯的东部，森林茂密，气温很高，火灾时有发生。当地人为了灭火，特地驯养了一支“大象消防队”。这个消防队由20头经过特殊训练的大象组成，每头象背上都驮着巨大的水桶。它们行动迅速，聪慧敏捷。每当森林发生大火，“大象消防队”便冲向火场，用长鼻子拉出水桶上的喷水管，打开放水开关。顿时，20个水龙头就向火场喷出粗大的水柱，大火很快就会被扑灭。

ELEPHANT FIREFIGHTERS IN AFRICA MOVE FAST

In the east of Tunisia, Africa, there is a large forest. The temperature is high, with constant fires. The local people trained 20 elephant firefighters, with giant buckets and pipes on their backs. They are swift and smart. When fire occurs, they come to the fire spot, pull the water pipes out and open the switch. The water flows from the pipe, and the fire is put out.

故事十八：训练小猪当警察，会用鼻子和蹄子

德国下萨克森州警犬学校的小猪，经过两个月训练就

能准确地从一个冰柜里找到曾经让它在别的地方嗅过的一瓶牛奶,九个月训练后,就能够隔着皮箱嗅出毒品,以后不久就能嗅出深埋地下一点五米深的毒品和作案工具。

在美国警队也有一支猪警察队伍。这些“警察”十分机敏,它们会用鼻子和蹄子,把发现的毒品挖出来。

PIG POLICE USES NOSE AND FEET

An army dog school in Lower Saxony Region in Germany trained little pigs in finding drugs and other crime tools with their noses. They can find the same bottle of milk it smelled before from many such bottles after two months of training, and find drugs buried 1.5 meters under the ground after nine months of training.

A pig police team also exists in the US police. These “officers” can use their nose and feet to dug out the drugs they found.

故事十九:维持秩序请鹦鹉,有人违规叫不停

美洲有一个城市的警察部门,为了节约人手,专门训练了一批鹦鹉到繁忙的街道上维持秩序,尤其是对付那些违反交通规则的人。当鹦鹉警察发现有人胡乱过马路或不走斑马线,它们就马上飞上前,对着那些行人叫个不停,直至他们遵守交通规则为止。

PARROT POLICE TRAFFIC GUIDERS SHOUTING TO TREPASSERS

A police department of a US city trained a team of parrots to keep the order on a busy street. When the parrot officer found anyone crossing the road, they would fly in front of that person and shout to them, until they walked according to the traffic rules.

故事二十：印尼有牛叫里贝，帮人渡河作工具

印度尼西亚有一种叫“里贝”的牛，体型比一般牛大，四肢极为粗壮，泅水能力很强。它泅水时，背部露出水面十分平稳。当地人在牛背上绑上一个不漏水的方形木盘，让人坐在上面，作为渡河的交通工具。

INDONESIA LIBEY COWS HELP PEOPLE CROSS RIVER

A kind of cow named Libey is larger than other cows. They have strong legs. When it is crossing a river, its back is steady above the water surface. The local people tie a large wooden plate to its back, so it can carry people across rivers.

故事二十一：非洲大蛇有力气，能拉 10 人渡大河

在非洲桑给巴尔西部地区的许多河口，当地居民过河时，大都使用一种大蛇为牵引力来摆渡。这种蛇，头部大，体力强，一次能拉一只载有 10 人的渡船过河。

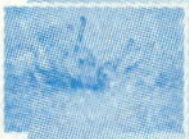

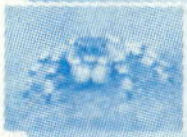

AFRICAN BOA CAN PULL A BOAT WITH 10 PEOPLE

There are many rivers of Zanzibar, Africa. When local people cross the river, they use a large boa to pull the boat. The strong boa can take a boat with 10 people across the river.

故事二十二：猴子领班管渡口，领头猴子讨渡钱

非洲扎伊尔境内，有个猴子管理的渡口，渡河工具是木筏，由一个老猴子领着七八只猴子充当船工，撑篙、摇桨全是猴子。中途如有人不慎落水，猴子们便跳入水里把人救上来。到了对岸，领头的老猴子就挨个向渡河的人讨渡钱。

MONKEYS IN CHARGE OF THE FERRY KNOW HOW TO CHARGE

In Zaire, Africa, there is a ferry in charge of monkeys. They use rafts to help people cross the river. A senior monkey leads seven or eight younger ones. They punt, paddle, and save people if anyone falls into the river. When they reach the other bank, the senior monkey will ask for money from those who took the boat.

故事二十三：非洲刚果有黄鳄，温驯载人渡江河

非洲刚果有一种温顺的黄鳄，当地群众常在交通不便的地方，使用这种驯服了的黄鳄作为渡河工具。方法是将树枝扎成渡架，平平正正地放在鳄鱼背上，由驯鳄的人驾驭渡河。

YELLOW CROCODILE PERFORMS AS BOAT IN CONGO AFRICA

Congo, Africa has a yellow crocodile with a mild temperature. Local people make a shaft from tree branches to put on its back, for people to sit on, and the crocodile trainer leads it to cross the river.

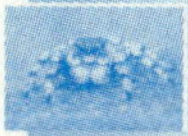

故事二十四：新加坡人驯养猴，采摘椰子知生熟

在新加坡热带海滨长着美丽多姿的椰子林，高达二三十米，浓密的树丛下挂着累累果实。椰子成熟了，当地人就培训黄毛猴上树去摘。新加坡养猴场驯养的黄毛猴，只有两三公斤重，却能听懂 25 个马来语单词，人们只要发出命令，它就飞快地爬到高大的树枝上，去采摘主人需要的花朵和果实。它两只后爪勾住树干，两只前爪摇晃枝上椰子，根据声响就能判断椰子的生还是熟，然后，就用力摘下熟椰子，既快又好。

MONKEYS TRAINED IN SINGAPORE HELPS PICK MATURE COCONUTS

Coconut trees grow in tropical coasts in Singapore. They are about 20-30 meters tall, with many fruits on the top. When the coconuts are mature, the local people train yellow monkeys to pick up the fruits. The monkeys weigh about 2-3 kilograms, and can understand about 25 Malaysian words. They can understand the orders, and pick up flowers or fruits demanded by their owners. They can even tell whether the coconut is mature by shaking it.

故事二十五：美国酒吧一老板，每日存款狗办理

美国林肯市一家酒吧间的老板阿伦，每天打烊后都要将这天的收入存入银行。令人惊奇的是，做这桩事的不是阿伦本人也不是店中的服务员，而是一只名叫“托比”的狗。

托比每天用嘴咬着钱袋跑到银行，像其他顾客一样排队等侯。轮到它时，它将两条前腿搭上窗口，把钱袋放在柜台上，由银行出纳员替这位“老主顾”填写存款单，办理存入手续。托比干这项工作已有一年半光景。当人们询问阿伦，何以让狗干这件事而不由人来干？他耸耸肩膀说，托比是只经过训练的狗，它从不误事，不会像有些人那样不可靠。

DOG IN CONTROL OF MONEY IN A US BAR

Ellen, the owner of a bar in Lincoln, US, put the revenue of the day in bank after closing. A dog named Toby helped him do so.

It put the purse into its month, and waited in line in the bank like the others. When it was its turn, it put the purse on the bank counter, and the cashier would fill in the deposit slip for the shop owner. Toby had been doing the job for more than a year. When people asked Ellen why he didn't give the job to a person, he shrugged and said Toby was trained, it would never fail him on the job, like some people would have.

故事二十六：澳大利亚众海豚，成为渔民好助手

澳大利亚沿海渔民，把海豚作为捕鱼助手。他们把一群海豚放在海湾里追逐鱼群，将它们赶向岸边，这样，渔民们不用出海就可以捕到鱼儿了。渔民们往往把捕到的一部分鱼分给海豚吃，作为酬劳。

DOLPHINS HELPED FISHERMEN IN AUSTRALIA

Fishermen near Australian coast take dolphin as their partners in fishing. They let the dolphins drive the fish near the coast, so that they don't need to go on the sea to fish. They spare a part of fish to the dolphins, as a reward.

故事二十七:圣地亚哥一餐厅,动物服务特温馨

智利圣地亚哥市有一家奇特的动物餐厅。餐厅里除了收款员和厨师以外,其余的服务员都是经过专门训练的动物。

当顾客一走进大门,门旁的两只鹦鹉立即热情地用英语、法语和西班牙语向顾客问好。接着,就有一只金丝猴殷勤地将客人脱下的衣帽挂进存衣室里。待顾客在桌前坐好后,一只温厚的长耳犬立即迎上前来,嘴里衔着菜单请顾客点菜。过一会儿,便有两只身材高大的长毛猴端上顾客买的食品和饮料。顾客用餐完毕,金丝猴会取来衣帽还给顾客,并端着一只盘子,收取用餐费用。

SANTIAGO RESTAURANT WITH ANIMAL WAITERS

Santiago has a special restaurant, where only the cashiers and cooks are human, and the waiters are all trained animals.

Two parrots greet the customers at the door in English, French and Spanish. Then a monkey takes off their coat and hat, and put the clothes into the cloakroom. After the customers are seated, a dog comes along and offers them the menu. Two big long-haired monkeys serve food and drink. After the meal, the monkey would return the clothes, and take the fee with a plate in its hand.

故事二十八：非洲丛林一旅馆，人身缠蛇为避暑

在非洲丛林深处有座世界上绝无仅有的蛇缠旅馆。这是因为在丛林中生活着一种无毒缠人蛇，它喜欢与人为伍，但绝不伤人，人也喜欢它。由于丛林酷热，它缠人身时，人会感到非常凉爽舒适。所以，旅馆的每个房间都用无毒缠人蛇作为避暑之用。

HOTEL IN AFRICAN FOREST OFFER SNAKE TWINING SERVICE

A snake hotel in African forest in forest is world's unique. In the forest lives a non-poisonous snake, which is a friend of people's. When it twists on human body, people feel cool and comfortable. So every room has the service of the twining snake.

故事二十九：偏远小岛有医生，训练信鸽送血样

法国有一个名叫约岛的偏远小岛上，仅有一名医生，

名叫安德雷克斯。他的诊所设备十分简陋，如果病人需要验血，就得将血液样本送到十六海里以外的一个岛屿，该岛上的实验室离约岛是最近的。为了尽快得到验血结果，安德雷克斯训练了一只信鸽。需要时，安德雷克斯将血液样本绑在信鸽的腿上，飞去交给那里化验员。两小时后，化验员便可将化验结果通过电话告诉安德雷克斯。

PIGEONS DELIVER BLOOD SAMPLES FOR DOCTOR

On a small island in France, there is only one doctor named Andrex. He doesn't have much medical equipment, so if his patients need a blood test, he has a pigeon send the sample to the nearest laboratory 16 sea miles away. Two hours later, people in the lab can telephone to inform the doctor the result of the blood test.

故事三十：内罗毕有大医院，治病患靠大乌龟

在肯尼亚首都内罗毕的一家现代化的大医院里，有一个特殊的“门诊部”。每天，“门诊部”前门庭若市，就医者络绎不绝。然而，在这里接待患者的不是医生，而是一只活的大乌龟。乌龟被拴在水池旁边的一棵树下。来这里就医的都是头痛患者。他们只要在龟背上坐上五分钟

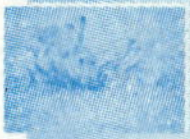

到半小时，头痛即可消失。

MODERN HOSPITAL IN NAIROBI TREATS WITH TURTLES

In a modern and large hospital in Nairobi, Kenya, there is a special department. Everyday many patients come to cure their headache. While the doctor there is a giant turtle under a tree near a pool. Only five minutes sitting on the back of the turtle can cure the headache.

故事三十一：北极狗充当向导，探险队化险为夷

北极狗个儿不大，身披浓毛，善于奔跑。暴风雪中要是迷了路，它有本事带领主人回家。

二十世纪初，有两个探险队远征南极，在鲸湾附近相

遇。阿蒙森探险队选择了一条较平坦的道路,以北极狗引路;而斯科特探险队选择了另一条迂回的路线,用马作交通工具。结果是:马和它的主人在暴风雪袭击下先后死去了;北极狗和它的主人却顺利地到达南极区,又平安地返回了基地。

ARCTIC DOG LED EXPEDITION OUT FROM DANGER

Arctic Dogs are not big, and with long hair. They are good at running. If their owners get lost in storm, they know the way home.

In the early 20th century, two expeditions went to the Antarctic Pole. They planned to meet each other near the Walvis Bay. Team Emerson chose a flat path with arctic dogs leading the way; Team Scott chose another detoured path, riding horses. At last, the horses and their owners died in a storm, while the dogs accompanied the other team to the Antarctic Pole, and then they traveled back safe.

故事三十二:纽约婚礼真新奇,9只小狗当傧相

美国纽约一对新人的婚礼,是由一群狗伴随着进行的。原来,新郎向新娘求婚时,新娘提出条件说:"要同我

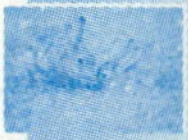

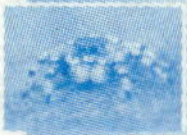

结婚，我的9只狗也必须一同陪嫁。"结婚那天，3只狗走在前面做向导，四只狗穿着盛装当傧相，一只狗头套花环跟在后面，还有一只叫"天使"的小狗沿途撒玫瑰花，给婚礼增添了新奇的风采。

A WEDDING IN NY WITH NINE DOG ATTENDANTS

A couple chose a herd of dogs to attend their wedding in NY. When the bride proposed, the groom said, "If I marry you, my nine dogs have to be together with us." So at the wedding day, three of her dogs walked before the couple, one followed with a flower ring on its head, another one scattered rose petals, and the other four attended with full suits. Thanks to them, the wedding was something to remember.

故事三十三：玻利维亚送奶鸟，分泌奶汁育婴儿

在南美洲的玻利维亚有一种奇特的鸟，雌鸟腹部有一奶囊，可以分泌出许多营养丰富的奶汁。当地人常以这种鸟的奶汁来哺育母乳不足的婴儿，因此这种鸟被称为"送奶鸟"。

MILKING BIRDS IN BOLIVIA NURTURES BABIES

A bird in Bolivia, South America is called milking bird, for their females can produce milk with the milk purse on its belly. Local people breed babies whose mothers don't have enough breast milk.

故事三十四：危地马拉气象鸟，预报天气好助手

危地马拉热带丛林里有一种鸟，能预报天气的变化。当天气发生变化之前，这种鸟会相应地发出各种不同的声音来表示将会有不同的天气状态。如叫声凶猛有力时，是表示将有一场很大的暴风骤雨；如叫声尖锐短促时，则表示这场风雨虽然来得很猛，但去得也急。

WEATHER BIRDS IN GUATEMALA

A bird in Guatemala tropical forest can forecast the changes of weather. Before the weather changes, it gives different sound to inform the local people. If it gives a strong and fierce voice, it means a heavy rain is coming; while if the voice is short and sharp, it means the rain will stop in a short time.

点评：

人类为了增加生活的乐趣和改善自己的生活质量去驯养动物；动物在服务人类的同时，也为自己的生存找到了依靠。动物服务人类是世界给予人类的丰厚礼物。大量的故事说明，这种服务并不完全是人类强加给动物的，也是自然界寻求平衡与发展的一种基本形式。动物在为人类服务的过程中，也同人与人之间的服务关系一样，有和谐的关系，也有冲突和不安。

People train animals for their own conveniences and fun. While serving people, animals found the meaning and support of their lives, too. Their service is a gift by nature. Stories show that the service is not enforced on them by human, but a form of balanced development in nature. In the process of the serving, there occurs different relations between human and animals.

十一 动物与人和谐相处的故事

Stories of a Good Relationship Between Men and Animals

故事一：和平相处二十载，人蛇互敬两依依

八十年代初，四川盆地地区某乡有一唐姓村民，他家只有几间简陋的草房，其中一间用来堆放柴草。

有一天，唐某抱柴生火，突然，一条白底黑花的大蛇赫然眼前。那蛇身有茶杯般粗，盘蜷着如一个米筛那么大。唐某想，蛇本是民间吉祥之物，不能随便猎杀，便听之任之了。此后，这位不速之客也就不客气地住了下来。日子久了，它不仅没有惹是生非，倒给主人家带来意想不到的好处。大蛇喜食老鼠，自它进了家门，唐家的老鼠很快就绝了迹。

一晃6年过去了，慢慢脱贫的唐某准备拆了草房建新房。拆房前，唐某来到大蛇窝着的柴草堆，郑重其事地

对大蛇说:“我要修新房了,你走吧,不然拆房时压着你……”大蛇似乎听懂了他的话,悄无声息地黯然游走了。

新土坯房修好后,唐某在房顶上以树木为梁放柴草。当天晚上,唐听到楼上柴草索索地响,他就知道,大蛇又回来了,说来也怪,唐某心里也突然变得安稳,好像久别的家人又回来了。

每年,当唐某从地里收回新的柴草,翻晾屋顶的草堆时,能看到它蜷缩在角落里,体型越来越大,性情温驯如初。

20 YEARS FRIENDSHIP BETWEEN VILLAGER AND SNAKE

At the early 1980th, a villager named Tang in Sichuan Basin region had a few shallow grass houses, one of them for piling up firewood.

One day when he came to the house for firewood, he suddenly saw a big white snake with black spots. It was as thick as a mug, and as big as a rice sieve when it curled up. Tang thought that snake is the lucky animal according to tradition, so he let it stay in his house. The snake didn't cause any trouble in the house, but ate up all the rats around.

Six years past, Tang became richer and planned to

tear down the grass house and build a new one. Tang said to the snake, earnestly, "I will tear down the house, you should go or it might hurt you." The snake seemed to understand him, and went away quietly.

After the new mud house was built, Tang used the roof to store firewood. In the evening he heard a rustling sound in roof, and he knew the snake was back. It was like a family member coming back.

Every year when Tang gets new firewood and dry the old one in sun, he sees the snake in a corner, larger every year, but mild as ever.

故事二:78 年人龟缘,世间多少不了情

1999 年 1 月 18 日傍晚,细雨绵绵,安徽省肥西县圩丁村 79 岁的丁同伦老人刚走出门,只见一只大乌龟正伸出头睁开圆溜溜的眼睛看着他呢。老人惊喜地蹲下身子,轻轻地捧起大乌龟,把它抱回家。这只大乌龟背部呈古铜色,肚子长满青苔,头部呈金黄色。腹部龟壳上"圩丁丁同庚"等字样清晰可辨。大乌龟身长约 34 厘米,身宽约 25 厘米,重约 3.8 公斤。

这只大乌龟是丁同伦的哥哥丁同庚 7 岁那年从集市上买回的,当时,这只乌龟仅巴掌大,浑身是伤。过了一

个多月，乌龟身上的伤痊愈后，丁同庚就在它腹壳部刻上了村名和自己的名字，然后把乌龟放了生。

第二年春天，这只乌龟突然爬进了丁同庚家。78年以来，除特殊年景外，乌龟几乎每年春天都回来一趟，每次回来，不是雨天就是雾天。大乌龟最后一次离别丁同庚是在1965年春。此后的十年时间里，大乌龟一直没有回来，同庚老人临终前，把弟弟丁同伦和儿子丁文仓叫到跟前说："大乌龟十年没有回来了，它肯定会回来的，我走了，你们可要善待有灵性的大乌龟啊！"

有一天，大乌龟在本属冬眠的季节，回到丁家，一待就是二十多天，吸引了成千上万的人来观赏。同乡的一位妇女向人们讲了这样一件事：十八年前，她的哥哥周某得到了这只大乌龟，他把大乌龟拿到菜市场去卖，人们看到龟壳上刻有很多字，知道这是一只年代久远的乌龟，没人敢买。就在这时，一个饭店老板对周某说："你如果把它的头割下来，我就买。"周某拿起刀，正欲割下它的头，这时，一辆从舒城来的货车撞了过来，周某当场死亡。周的侄女婿知道了这件事情，骑着摩托车从合肥赶到安庆，把大乌龟放入宽阔的长江里。放它的时候，大乌龟头翘得老高，不愿走，周的侄女婿说："我不能保护你，你走吧。"后来，大乌龟才依依不舍地走了。

1994年腊月，肥西县严店乡一位用电瓶打鱼的人把大乌龟打中，被一个叫钟祖保的人花了155元买回，第二天，钟祖保在大乌龟背上刻了“钟祖保三人放”，租车同三位朋友放生巢湖。

1999 年 1 月 26 日，太阳西斜，晚霞绮丽。丁同伦等人把大乌龟用小木桶拎到离家 300 来米的大坝放生。当他们把大乌龟放入水中时，它就是不走。丁同伦看到此，有点不舍地说：“你不愿意走，就回来吧！”大乌龟像得到命令的一般，马上调转头，爬了回来。之后，丁同伦又去大坝放生，闻讯赶来的群众有上千人。大乌龟还是不想走。主人只好将它又抱了回来。

78 YEARS OF FRIENDSHIP WITH A TORTOISE

It was a rainy dusk day in 1999, an old man named Ding Tonglun found a giant tortoise out of his door. The tortoise had copper-colored back, a belly covered by moth, and a golden head. It was about 34 centimeters long, 25 centimeters wide and weighed 3. 8 kilograms. On its shell were the words: “Freed by Ding Tonggeng in Weiding Town”.

The tortoise was bought by Ding Tonggeng, Tonglun’s brother when the later was seven. At the moment it was only the size of a hand, with many wounds. After it was healed, Tonglun freed it after he carved the words mentioned above.

The next spring the tortoise returned to Tonggeng’s

house, and came back almost every spring since then, in 70 or 80 years, all on rainy or foggy days. The last time it left Tonggeng was spring of 1965. Ten years after that, it didn't return. Before Tonggeng died, he told his brother Tonglun and his sons, that the tortoise would surely come back, and they should treat it well.

One day the tortoise did return again, and stayed for more than 20 days. Many people came to see it. A woman of the village told a story about it. 18 years ago, her brother Zhou got the tortoise. He took it to the market to sell, but no one dared buy it for the words carved on its shell but an owner of a restaurant. The owner asked Zhou to cut the head of the turtle, and just when Zhou was about to wave his knife, a truck suddenly came and killed him. When Zhou's cousin-in-law knew about the tortoise, he came from afar and tried to free it to the Yangtze River. The tortoise held its head high and was unwilling to go. Zhou said, "I cannot protect you, and you should be free." Then the tortoise went away.

In 1994, it was caught by a fisherman, and bought by a man named Zhong Zubao. Zhong freed it in Chao Lake the next day, after carving the words, "freed by

Zhong Zubao and other two".

Then we come back to a beautiful dusk 26th, Jan. 1999, Ding Tonglun and others managed to free it on the damn 300 meters away from home. It refused to leave, so Ding said, "If you are unwilling to leave, you can stay." It returned like understanding the words. He tried again another day, with thousands of people watching. It still didn't want to leave, so Ding had to let it stay.

故事三：珊丽海边救海豹，放生一年相见欢

在苏格兰的一个小海岛上，有一家小旅店，老板娘名叫珊丽。一天下午，沙滩的阳光特别明媚，珊丽在海边散步，远远看见一只小海豹误落渔网，拼命挣扎，越挣扎网绳勒得越紧，最后遍体鳞伤，血迹斑斑，奄奄一息。珊丽急步上前，解开渔网，把它抱回家为它治伤喂食。

在珊丽的悉心照料下，一个半月后，小海豹完全康复。珊丽用白漆在它身上写了“凯蒂”二字，便把它送回大海。一年以后，怎么也想不到，有一天清晨，她打开大门，赫然看到凯蒂卧在石阶上。小海豹一见昔日的救命恩人欣喜若狂，兴奋地不断拍打前肢，口中发出愉快的声音，仿佛是向珊丽表示热烈问候，感谢救命之恩似的。珊

丽惊喜交集，立即将凯蒂抱进屋内，设"宴"招待这位犹如远行归家的女儿似的小海豹，宾主极尽欢乐。

A SEAL CAME BACK TO THANK ITS LIFESAVER SHELLY

On an island of Scotland, there is a hotel run by Shelly. On an afternoon when walking on the beach she saved a seal wounded by the fish net. She took it home, fed it and treated its wounds.

The seal healed in one and a half month. Shelly painted the word "Katy" with white paint on its body, and sent it back to sea. One day after a year, when Shelly opened her door Katy was right on her doorstep, flapping her forelegs and giving a happy sound, like greeting its lifesaver. Shelly was overwhelmed with joy and surprise. She took the seal into her house and treated it, like it was her daughter coming back from afar.

故事四：母鸡生来有灵性，逗乐长沙一群人

一天，长沙居民谢建军的亲戚送给他一只母鸡。一进家门，母鸡就表现出通人性的特点，家人无论什么时候一叫唤，母鸡就乖乖地到那里蹲下，用尖尖的尾巴和两只脚支撑着身子；将它翻过来，让它两脚朝天躺在沙发上睡觉，它绝不会自己站起来，而是温顺地躺着，一动不动。直到主人发话“起床了”，它才会翻身“起床”。

母鸡的绝技是保持身体平衡。谢建军让母鸡停在没有开刃的剑刃上，然后左右上下均匀地移动宝剑，母鸡毫不惊慌，依然在晃动的剑上悠然自得。这只母鸡的精彩表演，经常给围观的男女老少带来快乐。

SMART HEN AMUSED THE CROWD IN CHANGSHA

One day a hen was brought to the house of a Changsha resident, Xie Jianjun, as a gift by one of his relative. The hen was very smart. When people called the hen, it would quietly crouch down. If they turned it around with its feet to the sky, it would keep the posture until the owner told it to "get up".

The hen was very good at keeping its balance. It could stand firmly on a sword while its master was moving it around. Its performance often brought joy to the people watching.

故事五:冰天雪地莫斯科,见证温暖人狗情

在莫斯科一个寒冷的早晨,四岁的伊万便离开了他的母亲。因为,可怜的孩子在那个家里找不到一丝温暖,母亲是个酒鬼,她只知道找酒喝,根本不管伊万的死活。小伊万开始了流浪生涯。

莫斯科的冬天特别寒冷,每年冬天的街上都会有人冻死。可怜的小伊万又很幸运,他很快找到了爱。但令人惊讶的是,收容他的是一群野狗。小伊万在野狗的帮助下,度过了两个寒冬。那些忠心不二的野狗不但用身体为小伊万保暖御寒,还使他免受街头无赖对流浪儿的欺负。只要有人接近小伊万,野狗马上就狂吠不止,又抓又咬,直到吓跑不速之客为止。巡警曾三次试图将小伊万带走,小伊万似乎铁了心要和野狗生活下去,他根本不愿离开颇通人性的野狗。野狗也是发疯的保护小伊万。原来,小伊万在受到保护的同时,一旦讨到食物,便分给他身边的野狗。他们再现了古代故事中,人狗狩猎合作、

共同求生的世界。

ICY MOSCOW WITNESSED WARM HUMAN-DOG LOVE

On a cold morning in Moscow, four-year-old Evan left his drunkard mother, who knew nothing but looking for wine. Having no warmth with him, Evan left the house.

Evan was lucky to find warmth soon, but the one who took him in was a herd of wild dogs. He survived two cold winters thanks to the dogs. They gave him warmth with their bodies, and kept him from the bully of the rogues on streets. They barked and bit, if anyone tried to get near him. The police tried to take Evan away from the dogs, but he was unwilling to leave them and so were the dogs because Evan could find them food. It was like the stories about the cooperation between human and dogs in ancient times.

故事六:苍龙大蛇会运米,三弃不离主人家

1998年夏,江苏省一户陈姓村民家里发生了一件奇怪的事情。家人发现自己家吃的大米,每天吃掉多少,第二天米桶就会补满多少,而且只会多,只是米饭吃起来有

股腥味。有一天晚上，他们发现家里有一条碗口粗的苍龙大蛇，就从它家里爬出去。不大一会，大蛇又爬了回来，只是满身沾满了大米。原来，它是爬到别人家以后，张开身上的鳞片往大米堆里一滚，鳞片里就沾满了大米，随即夹紧鳞片回到陈家，松开鳞片，将米抖落在主人家的米桶里。真相大白后，陈家怕蛇，又嫌大米腥味难吃，就想办法把这条大蛇送走。

第一次，他把这条大蛇诱进一条很大的蛇皮袋，装了足有大半袋，扔到路边田野里，可第二天它就回家了。第二次，它又把大蛇诱进蛇皮袋，走了数里路，过了一座桥，把它扔到一个木材市场，谁想到，第二天它又回家了。第三次，他决定把它扔到更远的山上去。未料到，过了两天，它又平安无事地回到了原地。看来这人蛇缘分未了，只能和谐相处了！

LOYAL BLACK SNAKE HELPED MOVE RICE AND REFUSED TO LEAVE AFTER ABANDONED

In summer of 1998, something strange happened in villager Chen's house, in Jiangsu Province: no matter how much rice they eat every day, the next day the rice will be reloaded, and it smelled raw. One night Chen found a giant black snake thick as a bowl in his house, and drove it away. Yet it returned a moment after, with rice all over it. Chen found out that it came to others' house, roll in their rice with its scales open, then close them so that the rice was left in its scale, and went back to Chen's house. Chen's family was afraid of the snake, and didn't want it to make the rice smell bad, so they tried to send it away.

One day he lured it into a bag and threw the bag to the near field, but it came back the next day. The next time he took it to a market miles away, while it came back again. The third time he took it to the hill farther away, yet it still returned in two days. It seemed that they had special relations with the snake, so they had to stick together in harmony.

故事七：打柴捡回两熊崽，两年养育情难舍

1997年3月，贵州省一个小镇的居民孟大发在上山打柴途中，无意中捡回一雄一雌两只各重约两公斤的黑熊幼崽。经两年多精心养育，这对黑熊"兄妹"，每只体重达到近150公斤，而孟大发为此付出的代价是欠债近3万元，妻子不堪重负离他而去。从小与人相处，使得这对庞然大物极通人性，成了孟大发和全村乡亲心中分量很重的宠物明星。每天闲暇之余，总有三三两两的村民围坐在孟大发家大院里，与黑熊嬉戏，抽烟聊天。城里的客

人们也慕名远道来到偏远的水头寨看黑熊。

BABY BEARS RAISED BY A FARMER

In March 1997, Meng Dafa, a resident in a town in Guizhou Province, found two baby black bears on his way back from wood-cutting, each weighted 2 kilograms. The "brother and sister" bears weighted about 150 kilograms each after two years staying with Meng. Meng raised the bears at the cost of 30,000 yuan's debt, and his wife's leave. The bears were very smart for they spent a long time with human. They became stars of the town. In leisure times, the town people gathered in Meng's house, smoking, chatting and playing with the bears. Many people even came to the distant town from cities, to visit the bears.

故事八:与蛇同眠如好友,人蛇奇缘世代传

在海南省有位青年农民黄某,在槟榔园劳作时发现一条身长不足一米、大拇指粗、体重不足半公斤的幼蟒。黄某见它可怜,便将它带回家。从此,他与蟒蛇同眠达三年,直到黄某结婚,才让蟒蛇住客厅。这条蟒蛇特别温顺,黄某三岁的儿子经常坐在蟒背上,像骑马一样和蟒蛇嬉戏。

AMAZING FRIENDSHIP WITH A BOA PASSING TO NEXT GENERATION

A young farmer Huang in Hainan Province, found a boa thick as a thumb when working in an areca garden. It was less than a meter long and less than half a kilogram. He took it home and slept with it for three years. When he got married, it moved to his dining room. The boa was mild in character. His 3-year-old son often rode on its back, just like riding a horse.

故事九:沼泽地里救灰鹤,腿伤治好不愿归

2003 年 6 月的一天,黑龙江省居民范某去山里采蕨菜,路过一片沼泽地时,听到不远处的草丛中发出凄厉的鸟鸣。顺着叫声,他找到了一只腿部受伤的小鹤,便抱回家中给它包好伤口。每天,他还去河里捞小鱼喂小鹤。十几天后,小鹤能站起来了。

看到小鹤一天天长大起来,范某在五个月的时间里,放飞了五次。但每次灰鹤都又飞回范家。灰鹤每天“看家护院”。邻居家的鸡跑进来,它就舞动着翅膀把鸡赶出去。灰鹤还是电视迷,每天晚上都和范家人一起守在电视机前看节目,荧幕前要有蚊子、苍蝇,它可毫不留情。

A GREY CRANE UNWILLING TO LEAVE ITS LIFESAVERS

A day on June 2003, a Heilongjiang resident Fan went to the mountains to pick some vegetables. He heard a sharp tweet from a bird near a marsh. He found a little crane with a wound on its leg. He took it back and bound up the wound. Every day he went to the river to get fish for it. After about half a month the crane could stand again.

In five months after that, Fan tried five times to let the crane go, but it returned every time after. It began to serve as guard of Fan's house, and drove away the chicken that ran into it. It was a fan of TV, every night it watched TV with the family. It never spared the flies or mosquitoes if they flew around.

故事十：买只小鸭有灵性，见人握手又敬礼

武汉市居民董元梅的侄女一天带了一只鸭子来看望她。董元梅老两口觉得鸭子太小，不忍心杀掉。没想到，两个月后，他们发现这只鸭子特别可爱，他们走到哪里，鸭子跟到哪里。由于老两口膝下无儿女，慢慢地，这只鸭子成了他们家的宝贝，闲来无事就逗它玩。

这只鸭子的确很聪明，见到董元梅老两口总是点头哈腰的"敬礼"，家里来了客人，董元梅要它给客人敬礼，它也很听话。后来，这只鸭子还学会了用嘴巴与人"握手"。

DUCK KNOWS BOWING AND HAND-SHAKING

Wuhan resident Dong got a duck from her niece as a present. Dong thought the duck was little, so she raised it instead of killing it. Two months later they found the duck become a cute pet. It followed them everywhere, and bowed every time when seeing them. Dong asked it to bow to her guests, and it did. Then it learned to "hand shake" with its beak.

故事十一：母猪为表养育恩，握手礼节从不废

鹤岗市的一个家庭养殖场里，有一头母猪。每次饲养员回来的时候，它都能感觉到饲养员的脚步声。一年多来，只要饲养员回到猪圈，好像为了表达对饲养员的谢意，它就会扶着墙站起来，和饲养员握手。

PIG SHAKES BREEDER'S HAND TO SHOW GRATITUDE

In a livestock farm in Hegang City, Heilongjiang Province, lived a female pig. It could tell the footsteps of its breeder. In more than a year, whenever the breeder came to it, it stood up with its feet against the wall, and shook hands with the breeder, just like it was showing its gratitude.

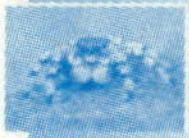

点评：

有位动物学家曾说过："人类最原始的艺术是对狗的驯养。"乌龟、灰鹤、猪、鸡、鸭等各种动物同狗一样，在人的驯养和接触过程中，它们同人也能建立和谐友爱的关系。善待动物，首先要善待自然；保护动物，首先要保护自然。由于人类的干扰，动物的群居环境正日益变得恶劣起来。在南美洲秘鲁的钦查群岛中，有一个小岛曾经是鸟的天堂，每天有六百多万只海鸟生息在那里。从1984年到1995年，秘鲁人在这个岛上开采的鸟粪就有二千多万吨。但是后来由于受人类砍伐树木和中美洲暖流的影响，1995年以后，这个显赫一时的鸟岛，很快就成了荒岛。事实上，只要人类不以"自然界的主宰"自诩，不要忽视甚至剥夺动物的生存权，善于与动物沟通、交流，给它们帮助、关爱，动物们也懂得尊重人类。只要人和动物和谐相处，我们的世界将会更加美好！

A zoologist once said, "The most ancient art of human was the training of dogs." Other animals, too, could have harmonious relationship with human. To protect animals, we must protect the nature. The habitation of animals is turning worse because of human's activities. In Chincha Islands of South America, an island was once the heaven of birds. Peru people got more than 20 million tons of bird waste

during 1984 to 1995. However, because of wanton felling of trees and the warm current from Middle America, the island turned into a wasted land soon after 1995. In fact, if people do not take themselves as the dominator of nature, do not ignore, or take away the survival right of animals, do help and communicate with them, they will respect us, too. If man and animals co-exist in harmony, the world will be better!

《走近动物》系列(中英文版)后记

《走近动物》系列(中英文版)的出版是我们历时数年品味自然、透视社会、领会人生的结晶。它的问世是一个漫长的历程,也是我们寻求家庭文化的一个重要里程碑。

八十年代中期,我们就试图建立一个能够作为家庭文化的田园。它既能增长知识,又是对人生的一种体悟和思索。于是,我们就像蓝天白云下耕耘不辍的农夫,除了在各种报刊收集一些最新的动物故事,还经常到街头的旧书摊去购买一些涉及动物方面的趣闻轶事。这些故事、奇闻和传说,虽然很难一一求证,但是大多数是有出处的。随着时间的推移,收集的素材越来越多,我们越来越强烈地感受到动物和人的联系是那样密不可分;同时,也使我们更加深刻地感受到人和动物和谐相处的重要。事实上,我们完全可以通过对动物世界的了解,从而更直接、更感性地去了解人性。1999 年,安徽美术出版社《动物传奇 1999》的出版和巨大的发行量给予我们极大的鼓舞。但是,它并没有实现我们所期望的目标,那就是让人们从动物世界的生存方式和生活形态中去透视人的自然属性,从而更好地认识自己,升华自己的社会属性。为此,我们开始对动物奇趣和动物问题的哲学思考,并且采

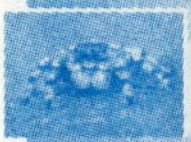

用“纪实文学”的手法，将我们所收集的、经历的、听到的各种有关动物的轶闻趣事进行分类、整理、编纂和创作，并富有创意的将这些异事、故事、奇闻和佳话，演变成一部具有深刻思想内涵的整体构架，以更淋漓尽致的展示动物同人类的联系和相近之处。

动物是人类的一面镜子，动物的行为对人类心灵的影响是显而易见的。考古学领域发现的动物活动的遗存都说明，动物是这个地球上早于人类的生命现象。在人类出现之前，动物们自在地生活在阳光之下，所有的争斗和厮杀，都是“物竞天择、适者生存”的需要。正如中国书协会员、中华诗词楹联学会会员齐飞先生在读后感中所说的，为了唤醒人们热爱动物的良知、自觉加入保护动物的行动和行列之中，作者试图找到一个人们更能接受的途径，让人们走近动物的生活，从而亲身感受动物的机智和灵活、天性和本能、简朴和纯粹。让人们在动物们的一个个传奇中，感悟自然的造化和神奇，反思人类的贪婪和无知。《走近动物》系列（中英文版）所包括的四个主题：《动物的爱情传奇》《动物的战争传奇》《动物的文明传奇》《动物的义举传奇》，都是实实在在地来自于生活中的发现；同时，也集中体现了人类最高的精神追求，即对真、善、美的渴望和期盼。

《走近动物》系列（中英文版）里有温情脉脉、凄婉哀

怨的动人和悲凉；也有弱肉强食、适者生存的骄傲与悲壮；更有扶弱济贫、仁爱和谐的义举和善良。我们试图用感性的文学素描手法去形象地表达某种观点，因为那样往往比通过理论抽象给人的印象要深刻得多，尤其是对孩子的魅力更是自然而然的。当人们还没有更好的方法来引导孩子们更快成熟起来的时候，应当说，《走近动物》是了解人生真谛最精彩，最生动的捷径之一！

当然，我们还希望把它作为一部学术著作来对待，毕竟它蕴涵着爱护自然、保护动物的思想火花！书中记载的每一个故事、奇闻、佳话和传奇也为动物学、心理学、生物学、人类学和哲学的研究提供了可资借鉴的素材。

安徽大学是我们的母校。“至诚至坚、博学笃行”的精神培育了我们的心智，增长了我们的知识，提升了我们的境界。在我们毕业30周年之际，能够在安徽大学出版社出版《走近动物》系列（中英文版），是一件非常有意义的事！感谢那些在该书的创作过程中，给予支持和帮助的动物保护人士和热衷探讨动物问题的专家、学者。

亲爱的朋友！当您漫步在充满智慧的动物文明乐园中、行在充满神奇的动物爱情王国里、驰骋在充满血腥的动物厮杀战场上、沉浸在充满友善的动物义举故事中之时，您一定会为动物的爱情和战争深受震撼和感动，您也一定会因动物的文明和义举深受震惊和感悟！

The Postscript of This Series of Books

The publication of this series of books Animal Legends was our fruit that after years' research on the nature, observation of the society and the understanding of the life. The process was quite long, and it was an important milestone of our family culture.

In the 1980's, we had tried to build a system of family culture which we could enrich our knowledge as well as realize and ponder about our life. We worked hard like the farmers in the field, we collect all the animal stories we could get from all kinds of magazines and newspaper, we bought relative books on the second-hand bookstores. The stories and legends were hard to be proved but most of them were real. As time went by, the connection between animals and human beings became stronger and stronger. It was more and more important to stay in harmony with animals. In fact, we could get to know the nature of human beings through the stories of animal world. In 1999, Anhui Art Publication Press had published *Animal Legends of 1999* , and the huge sales of this book did enlighten us up, but it failed to fulfill our target, which was to let

people know more about human nature through the stories of animal and get to know themselves much better, thus to improve the social attribute. Since then, we began to combine the animal stories with the philosophical ideas, we classified the stories and recreate them in a documentary way. The whole stories were turned into an overall framework with deep ideological contents by our creative work, in order to show the connection and likeness between animals and human beings.

Animal was a mirror for human beings. The influence of animals' acts to human minds is obvious. According to the study of archaeologists, animals appeared much earlier than human beings. Before the birth of humans, animals lived a harmonious life in the colorful world. They obeyed the law of the nature that was natural selection, survival of the fittest. As Mr. Qi Fei, the member of Chinese Writing Association and the Chinese Poems and Couplets Association, said in the reader's response that the author tried to find a receivable way to let people get near to animals' lives, feel their intelligence and flexibility, natures and

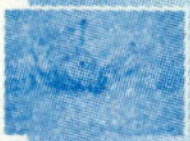

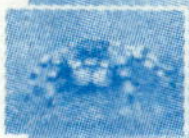

instincts, purity and simpleness. This series of books contained four themes: love, war, culture and hero. The themes were extracted from animal life, it showed the highest pursuit of human beings as well, which was the pursuit for truth, goodness and beauty.

This series of books had moving stories, great wars, and the kindness acts by animals. We tried to describe our points of view in a sensitive way, for that was easier for people to memorize and understand than theories, especially for children. I believed that this series of books were a shortcut for people to understand the truth of life.

Of course, we hope that readers could treat this series of books as academic works for it contains the thoughts of protecting the nature and animals. The stories offered valuable materials for researches from all aspects.

Anhui University was our alma mater, we bear the motto in our minds "Be honest and strong, rich in knowledge and tenacious of purpose". It was a memorable thing for us to publish this series of books in Anhui University Publication Press on the 30th anniversary of our graduation. At last, we would like to thank all the people who had given a helpful hand to us during the publication of this series of books!

My dear friends, when you were enjoying the world of smart animals, the romance of the animals, the battleground of theirs and their heroic stories, were you moved by them? I believe that you would enjoy the reading!

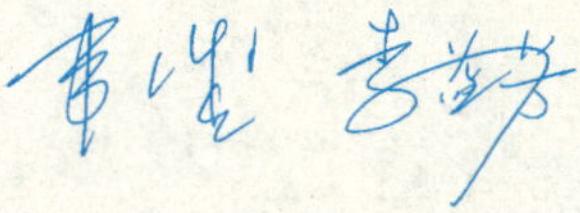

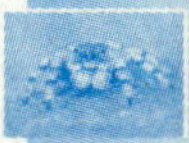